M000219653

TRUDGE:
Surviving the Zombie Apocalypse

SHAWN CHESSER

Copyright © 2011 Shawn Chesser

All rights reserved.

ISBN: 978-0-9913776-9-5

SHAWN CHESSER

ACKNOWLEDGMENTS

For Mo, Raven, Caden and Penny, who is now flying up in Cat Heaven. Thanks for putting up with me clacking away at all hours. Mom, thanks for reading… although it is not your genre. Dad, aka Mountain Man Dan, thanks for your ear and influence. Thanks to all of the men and women in the military serving our country, especially those of you in harm's way. All of my friends and fellows, thanks as well. Cover by Jason Swarr of Straight 8 Photography. Nice job!

Lastly, thanks to Bill W. and Dr. Bob… you helped make this possible. I am going to sign up for another 24.

Extra special thanks to Mo Happy for taking Trudge and polishing its many rough edges. Her input and insights have allowed me to publish this novel with pride.
Thank you Mo!

*****

Edited by Monique Happy Editorial Services
http://www.indiebookauthors.com

TABLE OF CONTENTS

Prologue
Day 1 - Portland, Oregon

It was a beautiful sunny Saturday morning in Portland, Oregon. Contrary to popular belief, it didn't rain here all of the time. It looked like a long hot summer was in store. Mount Hood towered in the east, white with snow year round. As they neared the airport, Cade pointed out to his daughter Raven the remnants of Mount Saint Helens visible to the north.

Brook wanted to have conversation time before being dropped off at the American Airlines departure area so they drove with the stereo off.

"Hey honey, while Raven and I are away, are you going to tackle the tile in the downstairs bathroom? Or are you and Ted going to tackle the Mariners' game at the pub?" Brook asked jokingly. She was fully aware of the plans her husband had made with their neighbor Ted. Cade was no slacker, Brook was just being playful.

"Mom, give Dad a break. He's driving. Didn't you know that the number two cause of automobile accidents is because of distracted drivers?" Raven said, her brunette pigtails bouncing as she turned her head and gave her mom a semi-serious stare.

"Yeah, listen to your factoid spewing daughter," Cade said as he glanced over his shoulder to check his blind spot before taking the next exit.

"Just so you two can squirm while you're away, I'll let you know exactly what I'll be doing. I am going to watch sports in my underwear, leave the toilet seat up the entire time and drink straight out of the milk carton." In the Grayson household these things were

1

usually punishable by at least ten minutes of nagging. Cade had gotten his one dig in and he left it at that.

He maneuvered the silver Toyota Sequoia to the curb and engaged the caution flashers. A tall gangly man sporting a ball cap and a dark blue American Airlines uniform complete with faux gold shoulder epaulets opened the rear hatch of the truck. While Brook filled out the baggage forms, Cade helped wrestle the six bags onto the porter's low slung cart. He peeled off a ten dollar bill and handed it to the man and thanked him.

Cade grabbed his petite wife and equally small daughter in a two armed bear hug. "I am really going to miss you guys," he said while he locked eyes with his wife for a moment. He had fallen in love with her big brown doe eyes at first sight many years ago. Brook was petite but her personality was enormous. She was the type that never backed down from anything or anybody. She had been an avid mountain climber years ago; now that she was in her mid-thirties she put all of her energy into raising her only daughter.

Their daughter Raven tended to be cautious, neither a leader nor a follower. A big researcher, she thought most things over many times before taking action, whether it was choosing which cereal she would eat that particular morning or which boy in sixth grade received her attention. She was a very cerebral girl and yet she still believed in the Easter Bunny.

After hugs and kisses, Cade got in the truck and pulled from the curb. He stole one long last look at his family as they entered the large revolving door and disappeared into the maw of the airport.

Halfway home he turned on the stereo and picked a classic rock station. The deejay was going on about a new mutant strain of H1-N1 that was making people sick in Washington D.C. It was the last thing he wanted to listen to on a worry free weekend. Monday would be bad enough. It was time to start the job hunt he had been putting off. It had been more than a year since he left the military with an honorable discharge. The economy was in tatters, unemployment was high and he knew the job offerings would be slim, so for now he chose to live in the moment.

As he merged into the light traffic moving on I-205 he pushed the AUX button on the stereo and picked up his IPod Nano. He rapidly shook the electronic device and let shuffle decide which

2

song he would get to listen to. He grinned when the first sitar riffs of the Doors' song *The End* emanated from the speakers and then sang along with Jim Morrison for a few prophetic verses.

He was blissfully unaware of the situation now unfolding in the heart of Portland.

Chapter 1
Day 1 - Portland, Oregon

Cade pushed the remote button on the rearview mirror and the garage door responded by starting to slowly open. He overshot the driveway by a few feet and reversed his truck up the driveway and into the two car garage. He walked into the house through the mudroom and deposited his keys on the top of the dryer. Before he entered the kitchen he removed his shoes, then pressed the glowing button on the wall. The garage door started on its downward journey. The house still smelled of bacon from the morning meal. The home felt very tomblike without his wife and daughter flitting about. The early morning sunlight streamed in between the horizontal slats of the blinds bringing a small semblance of warmth inside.

The flashing red light on the answering machine steadily pulsed. He strode across the room, and against his better judgment pushed the play button. Ted's voice sprang forth from the tiny speaker.

"Hey buddy, Ted here. I've got bad news and good news. Lisa is dragging me downtown to eat breakfast. She wants to go to the Saturday Market and then do some people watching in the Square. The good news is when we get back, I have the green light to go to the pub to catch the second game of the Mariners' double header. Call me later." Cade smiled to himself, then erased the message and got a bottle of water from the fridge.Cade's plush leather recliner beckoned. He planned to sit down for just a few minutes, but found himself dozing on and off. Hours later he was awakened by his ringing cell phone. After fumbling to retrieve the annoyance from his pants pocket he looked at the display. It was Brook calling from her mom's in Myrtle Beach. Trying to shake the cobwebs from his head, he groggily answered, "Hello?"

"Hi honey, we made it OK. Carl just dropped us off at Mom and Pops."

"How was the flight?"

"Smooth flight, awful food. You know, how it usually is."

"How did Raven do?" Cade asked.

"She slept the entire flight… I was amazed."

"Put her on, please."

After a moment Raven cheerfully answered. "Hi Dad, what's up?"

"I just wanted to make sure you take good care of Mom for me, OK?" He liked to instill as much self confidence in her as he could. A little esteem building went a long way.

She answered enthusiastically, "No problem Dad. Nothing shall befall my Mom when I'm on the job." She put the phone in Brook's outstretched hand after saying bye to her dad.

"I almost forgot to tell you. Pops is coming home from the hospital early. Something happened at work and he's not feeling well. I think Mom said he was bitten by a delusional patient."

"Keep me informed. I have got to get ahold of Ted and borrow some of his tools. I want to work on the bathroom before you guys return. Have a great trip. I love you. Give your parents my love too. See you soon."

Like always, Brook had the last words. "I love you too. Don't worry, I'm sure Dad is going to be just fine. He's a doctor for Christ's sake. Bye honey."

With that they both hung up.

Cade read a few pages of the latest Brad Thor novel before he got up off of his butt to change into his work clothes. Decked out in his Levis, tee shirt and tennis shoes, he decided to walk around the corner and pop in on Ted and Lisa unannounced.

Cade considered Ted and his wife Lisa good neighbors and even better friends. Brook and Lisa had been known on occasion to visit the local Starbucks together for a latte. Ted and his wife also hosted a yearly neighborhood block party every summer, which the Graysons made a point not to miss. With Brook and Raven out of town Cade hoped to finish the tile job in the bathroom. No better time to shorten the honey-do list than when the girls were out from underfoot. Ted had an industrial tile saw Cade needed to borrow.

One block from Ted's house Cade saw a man staggering down the street away from him. *Pretty early in the afternoon to tie one on,* crossed Cade's mind as he rounded the corner.

There was no answer when he rapped on his friend's front door. Since Ted's truck was in the drive, Cade tried the garage around back. Ted had an old Hunter Green MG sports car he liked to work on in his spare time; Cade assumed that's what he was doing.

Nearing the garage, he heard some noises coming from within and decided to sneak a peek and see what Ted was doing. Cade silently stole a look into the open side door. To his horror, he saw Ted with his face buried fully inside Lisa's exposed rib cage. Cade didn't want to believe what he was seeing. There was blood pooling all around her prone body and Ted's hair was slick with her bodily fluids.

"Ted, what the hell are you doing?" Cade growled furiously. In the next moment, something he would never forget greeted him. Ted's bloody face, with a mouth full of dripping innards, looked directly at him with a blank, "no one is home" stare. Exhibiting very little dexterity, what used to be Ted arose and jerkily started shuffling around the car in Cade's direction. Snapping back to reality he thought, *whoever this thing is, it sure isn't Ted.*

While searching for anything to use as a weapon, Cade spied a helmet and crampons on a shelf to his right. Finally he found what he was looking for. Hanging by a leather strap, next to the other gear, was a mountaineering ice axe.

Just as he grabbed it from the hook on the wall, Ted, mouth agape and moaning, lunged for his turned back. Quick reflexes helped him avoid the attack. All in one motion he spun around and buried the axe under Ted's sternum directly into his heart. It had no effect. The thing he used to call his friend kept clawing for his face.

From personal experience, he knew the blow should have killed any man. He put his tennis shoe clad foot on Ted's chest and pulled the blood slickened axe free, sending his neighbor sprawling into his low slung project car.

He aimed his next blow for the top of the creature's head. Its skull collapsed with a pop, and the dead weight rolled off of the car and impacted the concrete face down with a sickening crack.

On the other side of the MG, he saw the full scope of Ted's attack. He had feasted on his wife's abdomen, neck and all of the soft fleshy bits on her face. Lisa used to be a pretty woman, but now she was appalling to look at.

There was no holding back; the vomit came up in waves. Nothing he had seen in combat operations all over the world could trump this spectacle. Cade had killed plenty and witnessed even more death. Barging in on Ted cannibalizing his wife was a surreal experience. Having to kill him was inconceivable.

As Cade sat on the hard concrete floor pondering his deed and wondering what to do next, Lisa began to twitch. Turning her head ever so slightly, her lidless eyes honed in on him. As she arose, with few muscles left to support it her neck listed to the side nearly resting on her shoulder. She moved faster than he anticipated, teeth clicking, trying to take a bite of him.

He scrambled to his feet still brandishing the ice axe. Keeping his center of gravity low he worked his way around the little MG. The ghoul that was once Lisa followed steadily after. He rounded the hood of the car, planted his feet and waited for the abomination to get within reach. She lurched nearer, her claw-like hands reaching for his neck. With blinding speed, Cade plunged the ice axe into her temple. All of her compromised motor functions ceased and she crumpled to the garage floor.

Cade put some distance between him and the two dead bodies. His mind raced as he asked himself what had just happened.

There was a cordless phone hanging on the wall next to the side door. Cade put the phone to his ear but there was no dial tone. Calling the police was what he had aimed to do, but at this point his only option was to leave and sort it out later.

With the running water as hot as he could stand, he washed the bodily fluids from his hands into the utility sink. Mesmerized by the rivulets of bloody water slowly spiraling down the drain he thought his options through. *Ted and Lisa's bodies will have to stay where they fell. It would do me no good to mess with the... I almost said 'crime scene.' I need to remember what I did was purely self-defense. Something wasn't right. Lisa had to have been dead before she stood back up.* It brought back memories of the young insurgent in the Shah-I-Kot valley in Afghanistan that had absorbed a full magazine worth of bullets. He had somehow gotten right back up and then made it ten steps before falling dead. This was a very different situation. That terrorist had been jacked up on drugs and adrenaline. He was no expert, but judging by the amount of blood on the floor, Lisa had definitely bled to death while Ted was eating her.

Still stunned by the recent turn of events he decided to head for home. He would make another attempt to call the authorities and then his wife Brook when he got back to his house.

With troubling thoughts still weaving through his brain he exited the garage. His shoes left bloody splotches on the drive as he set out for his street.

The adrenaline still coursing through his body, his senses were now attuned to every sight, sound and smell. Distant sirens blared from multiple directions; the smell of smoke was in the air. It also just occurred to him that he hadn't heard any airplanes all afternoon. Cade's home was just a few miles from the airport and frequent over flights were normal. He also had a sixth sense tingle telling him there was more to this than his neighbor suddenly turning homicidal and cannibalistic.

Cade realized he was still holding the ice axe as he trudged up his front walk. What a sight that would be to responding officers, if he had been able to get hold of any. He sat down heavily on the stoop and fished his cell phone from his pocket. When he tried to make a call, all he heard was static. Inside the house the result was the same with the land line. He began to worry, and that sixth sense was now jangling discordantly.

Cade turned on the television for the first time since his family left. He selected one of the local news stations. The previously recorded footage was from Pioneer Courthouse Square, also known as Portland's Living Room. They were covering an impromptu rally that happened earlier this morning. The pierced, tatted, black-clad anarchists were stirred up. They were rallying against the government and everything else they weren't happy about. Judging by the signs and placards the protesters carried, they believed the mutated H1-N1 virus being reported was man-made. Beyond a shadow of a doubt they were convinced the government had released it on the unsuspecting "sheeple." Their theory was that the government would be "forced" to intervene, thus giving "The Man" more power and total control when martial law was eventually declared. They feared that Homeland Security and FEMA wanted it implemented to restrict the rights of the American population. Paranoia was rooted deep in anarchist circles.

Cade noticed uneasily that the police and National Guard had a heavier presence than usual for one of these gatherings.

While the reporter was telling his audience about the damage these same thugs had caused last year at the WHO conference, a huge opening suddenly appeared in the middle of the hundred plus anarchists occupying the center of the brick square. It looked like a fight had started within the crowd. As the human sea parted, two figures on the ground arose and started grabbing and biting anyone within reach. The footage lasted four or five minutes. During that time, many more joined the first two attackers and panic swept the rest of the crowd. Police and guardsmen stood dumbstruck as the bloody melee escalated. Guardsmen fired the first warning shots over the heads of the frantic, out-of-control throng. Their gunfire merely attracted the attention of the newly infected.

Cade stood transfixed by the scene on the screen as the troops started shooting their M4 rifles into the surging group of rioters, infected and innocents. Newly turned undead were now attacking soldiers and the gawking bystanders standing near the outskirts.

Pioneer Courthouse Square became the flash-point for the outbreak in Portland.

Within minutes there were so many wounded and dead they had to be transported not only to the closest hospitals downtown but to the suburbs as well. As Cade learned later, this created satellite centers of infection and helped it spread faster and further from Ground Zero.

The recorded footage ended and the station ran a snippet reporting violence and cannibalism at the Alamo in San Antonio. There were scores of deaths and hundreds of casualties there as well. The pace of news coming in was frenetic. Abruptly the station went to a live feed from a nearby hospital.

The petite brunette news lady from Channel 8 had just arrived on scene at Providence Hospital, and was reporting live. Behind her the emergency room was overcrowded and hectic. Nurses, doctors and other personnel were performing triage or actively attending to the injured. In the background four hospital workers hovered around an ambulance gurney, working on a man with horrible lacerations crisscrossing his face. One person continually did chest compressions. On three different occasions one of the four workers hollered "clear," and everyone stood back as the paddles were placed on the man's chest and he was administered an electric shock. His heart failed to restart. A short time passed and then they pulled a thin white sheet over the man.

The news lady continued talking about the large number of patients suffering from bite wounds and head trauma from the "Riot in the Square" as it had been dubbed by the media.

Cade watched intently as the camera panned left and zoomed in on the twitching, sheet covered man on the gurney. He sat up, the sheet cascaded from his upper torso, revealing his body, pale and bruised from death's onset. Sluggishly he turned only his head, his lifeless staring eyes fixating on the woman reporter.

Cade wanted to yell and warn the woman on the television but he knew that would be futile. Before the cameraman could react, or anyone else in the busy trauma center noticed, the risen corpse had planted two bare feet on the avocado green linoleum floor and covered the short distance to the unsuspecting anchor lady.

Wondering why she no longer held the shocked cameraman's undivided attention, she paused mid-sentence, glaring at him. The ghoul opened its mouth wide and attached itself to her neck on live television. A crimson fan of blood pulsed, spraying in front of the still recording camera. It had all taken place in a matter of seconds.

Hospital security guards rushed the attacker and wrestled him to the ground. He thrashed about wildly, hissing and moaning, mouth snapping. The guards and orderlies had their hands full. The newly turned corpse summoned enough strength to inflict bite wounds on two of the men struggling to subdue it.

While the tussle ensued in the background, the veteran reporter lay face down, spread-eagled, and bled to death. The grisly scene was broadcast live in full HD, on thousands of televisions.

The image on the screen switched from the live remote feed to the ashen, stunned and speechless anchors in the studio. A male reporter stammered and said a few words about his fallen co-worker before he scrubbed his hands across his face and visibly composed himself. The network promptly went to commercial.

It was astonishing that the cameraman had failed to warn the news reporter before her graphic demise had been captured on the live feed. Cade scanned the other news channels and saw that violence was breaking out in other cities. He was astounded as he watched people stand rooted, overwhelmed by fear as the infected overran them. Their fight or flight impulses were switched off by the improbable scenario their eyes and brain were still trying to register.

Chapter 2
Southeast Portland

Cade didn't sleep at all that night. He was worried sick for his wife and daughter. For the first few hours after the sun had gone down he kept watch out of Raven's upstairs bedroom window. The trickle of undead ambling up and down his street had increased. After closing all of the curtains and extinguishing the lights he tried to sleep. Every time he closed his eyes he saw his dead neighbors. Finally Cade got out of bed, dressed and went downstairs. He didn't want to but he was drawn to the television. He turned it on and watched all night. So far, the satellite hadn't failed. He didn't want to rely on the Portland news anchors for all of his information, given the incessant, high-strung babble and hyperbole coming from them since their colleague's death.

At first the cable news channels were no better. CNN, FOX and MSNBC were reporting that the outbreak was similar to SARS or H1N1. Their idea of useful information included the use of face masks, plastic sheeting and duct tape to secure against an airborne pathogen. All of the other alphabet news stations were the same. Speculation, guessing and second guessing passed for news. Tensions were at their highest as nations pointed fingers and missiles at each other. Threat levels were raised and armies mobilized. The only consensus was that the origin of the pathogen was still unknown, and every nation's survival depended on quick thinking and immediate action.

Cade noticed so far Portland as well as the central Rockies and Colorado weren't being mentioned very much in the news. The massacre in the Square was only big news locally.

Looking at the big picture, the world was in a mess of trouble.

Chapter 3
Day 2 - Portland, Oregon

As dawn broke revealing a bluebird-colored sky, a sortie of F-15E Strike Eagles from Portland International Airport roared overhead. They were on full afterburner and flying very low. Windows rattled and car alarms were triggered by the over flight. Two of the fighters peeled off and climbed higher and then resumed CAP (combat air patrol) in a circling series of laps over the city.

Cade remembered that in the days following the 9/11 attacks, there was a constant rumbling of National Guard fighter jets on CAP over Portland. It was apparent things had deteriorated very rapidly overnight.

Not being able to contact his loved ones or any of his other neighbors forced him to make the decision to leave the house and reconnoiter the neighborhood. Cade went out into his backyard, stepped up into an old rusty wheelbarrow, poked his head over the top of the fence and slowly scanned the alley left to right checking for any of the walking dead.

After concluding he was alone, as quietly as possible he eased his aluminum mountain bike over the six foot wooden fence that enclosed his back yard. Getting around on the bike would be faster than on foot and quieter than a car.

He vaulted over the fence to join his bike and crouched down, then inhaled and exhaled through his nose several times. The air smelled of smoke mingled with the distinctive stench of decaying flesh. The odor was most likely from one of his many dead neighbors he had observed ambling about the streets over the last day and a half.

Still crouched down, he swiveled his head slowly, intent on picking up any sounds coming from the grass and dirt alley that ran between the block of houses in the rear. With the back of his hand he wiped the sweat forming on his brow. He didn't detect any sounds nearby. In the distance a siren wailed.

Since the start of the outbreak the traffic on his street had dwindled to nothing, and the undead began appearing in larger numbers. The neighborhood had become eerily quiet except for the raspy moans of the walking dead. When one of them spotted anything living they would begin their low pitched moaning and alert the other walkers within earshot. It was akin to how dogs started barking at night, one starts howling and soon a string of baying dogs would all join in on the chorus.

In the big sandbox in the Middle East, situational awareness and constant training was what kept him alive. It was especially important now given the fact the dead were walking the streets. Cade knew they greatly outnumbered him; therefore he was very careful to avoid any contact.

Cade was an average sized man. With the exception of his intense hard eyes, he didn't look like a Tier-One Operator. Most of the soldiers he had trained with and gone to war with looked unassuming as well. There were a few of the moose sized, action star lookers in the teams. During operations they usually paid the price and humped the big guns.

Until fifteen months ago Cade was in country in the "Stan" (short for Afghanistan), hunting HVTs, foreign fighters and al-Qaeda terrorists. After about thirty or so, he had stopped counting the men he had sent to paradise.

Cade travelled light during his neighborhood excursion. His aim was to check out his surroundings and determine if he should shelter in place or bug out.

He wore khaki heavy duty workpants, a black long sleeve tee shirt and a well-worn black Trailblazers ball cap covering his dark, short cropped hair. A pair of black wraparound Oakley sunglasses shielded his eyes. Sturdy, steel toed black leather Danner boots protected his feet. Strapped to his left upper thigh was a semi-automatic 9mm Glock 17 and under his right armpit was a compact semi-automatic 9mm Glock 19 in a quick draw Bianchi holster. Both pistols were polymer, very light and dependable. Within easy reach in a nylon pouch on his belt were four extra, seventeen round magazines. A Gerber Mark-II combat dagger, ten inches of double bladed, hardened black steel, hung upside down from his combat harness. In his free hand he held the lightweight titanium ice axe. It had been worth its weight in gold during his first encounter with the undead. An hour spent with a rasp and file honed the points and blade of the axe razor sharp. Cade knew this was going to be a very effective and quiet weapon.

Even though he was more than a year removed from the Special Forces, he still possessed the tools of the trade; and had not forgotten how to use them.

Chapter 4
Day 2 - Southeast Portland

Straddling the bike, he secured the axe to the frame and rode quietly westward down the alley past his former neighbor's back fence. Two blocks into the ride he noticed the sickly sweet smell of death. Cade dismounted his bike to seek out the source. Cautiously glancing around the corner, he saw them. One was a balding black man, ashy and gray with sunken jaundiced eyes. Above his collar was a bruised and bloody gaping neck wound with dangling streamers of flesh that left muscle, veins, sinew and white vertebrae exposed. The only thing appearing to hold his head on was a blood soaked necktie. Blackish dried blood fully coated the front of the ghoul's three-piece suit.

Next to him was a small black woman with no visible wounds. She was undead also. Her formerly pastel yellow bathrobe was now thoroughly congealed with drying blood. Dirt, twigs, hair and all manner of refuse clung to the fabric.

Both of the undead were circling around the base of a large oak tree, hands in the air, reaching, mouths working like two macabre marionettes.

Cade assessed the situation from a distance. Upon further scrutiny he noticed a milled lumber platform about twelve feet off the ground, with a coiled up rope ladder attached. It was a tree house partially hidden by the lower boughs and leaves of the old oak.

There was some movement in the middle branches of the tree.

The two undead noticed it as well and started to moan. Barely audible over the chilling sound, a voice yelled, *"Help, up here!"*

The undead were oblivious to Cade's presence. Their attention was fully focused on the tree and the meat in it.

Taking advantage of the diversion, he crept up on the male cadaver from behind and to the right, being careful to stay shielded from Bathrobe's view. Three feet away from the undead businessman, he raised the sharpened ice axe in his right hand shoulder high and swung it in a wide horizontal arc at the creature's head. Brackish black liquid and putrid gray matter exploded from the baseball-sized hole in its temple. The dead executive collapsed instantly and the ice axe slipped from his head.

The heavy thud of the body colliding with the ground alerted the other ghoul to Cade's presence. Hissing and biting, she turned and lurched towards him.

In one fluid movement Cade sidestepped her lunge, drew his Gerber left handed and buried the dagger handle deep into the thing's eye socket. Her flailing arms were unable to get a purchase on him as she slumped towards the base of the tree.

After a quick wipe off on the grass, he put the dagger back in its sheath.

Cade felt something soft and wet squish under his boots. Looking down, he was sickened to see a mound of human-looking remains. Ribs, a spinal column, and scraps of skin, tendon, and flesh and blood lay in a greasy pile on the grass.

Cade was examining the remnants when a high-pitched voice from above shouted a warning, "Watch out behind you!"

Faster than an Old West gunslinger, the Glock was out of the Bianchi shoulder holster and in Cade's left hand. The pistol barked twice in rapid succession. The lethal double tap removed the frontal lobe and most of the elderly man's forehead and skullcap. As he fell towards the other two undead bodies, the remaining contents of his cranium painted the ground. The walker was wearing bloody night clothes and clutched a newspaper in its hand. Numerous bite wounds were evident on its arms, face and neck.

"Shooooot. It's old man Bandon. He was one of them too?" said the faceless voice in the tree house.

Gunfire was guaranteed to attract the dead. As if on cue their eerie moaning started to reverberate from blocks around.

"Get down here," Cade said, pausing to scan the surroundings. After a lack of response from above, he barked, "If you want to live let's go... *now*."

Two frightened faces peered down from the tree house. The ladder rapidly unfurled and they nearly clambered over each other trying to reach the ground.

At the first sight of the gory pile of remains, the younger of the two blurted out, "Missy's dead." He started crying, snot running down his upper lip.

Thinking the worst, Cade asked the boys if Missy was their sister.

The older boy tearfully choked out, "No... Missy was our cocker spaniel."

Glancing down, Cade was at the same time relieved and momentarily at a loss for words. Then he barked instructions at the two. "Follow me, be quick, but be quiet."

The older boy grabbed the younger one around the neck and hustled him by the three corpses at the base of the tree, all the while struggling to shield him from the scene using his hands. He wasn't successful in keeping his younger brother from seeing the bodies of the undead. Tearing away from the older boy, the younger one dropped to his knees and gave forth a guttural wail. "Mom... Dad..."

Cade knelt down and placed his arm around the young boy's shoulder.

The boy fought off the embrace, landing a fist on the stranger's temple. "*You killed them!*" the younger boy screamed, spittle flying from his mouth.

Cade grabbed the boy in a bear hug. He was hoping to calm him down enough to talk the kid's mind around what he had just witnessed. But also he was seeing stars from the sneak attack and needed a brief respite. The shot he took to the temple was perfectly aimed and had rung his bell.

The boy finally stopped struggling after some quiet, calming words from his brother.

Cade kept his grip firm and whispered into the young boy's ear. "I don't blame you for reacting the way you did. You need to

19

understand something though. I am truly sorry for what I did, but as hard as it is to believe, they were already dead." He paused for a moment to think before finishing out loud. "Why don't you guys help me understand what happened this morning." Cade released the boy.

The skinny, younger boy spoke first. "When Mom came home from graveyard shift at the hospital she started fighting with Daddy. They fight a lot but this was the worst ever. We usually just get out of their way until they chill."

"I hustled Ike up into the tree house. We thought we'd wait until they calmed down," the older of the two added. "Things got real quiet for a while and then we decided to go back into the house. I opened the screen door and it squeaked like it always does. The next thing I see is those," he said while pointing at his dead parents.

Cade told the two boys what he had learned, "It's all over the news. A virus or something is making people die and then come back to life or un-death, or whatever; they only want to eat. You, me, your dog... anything living... they don't discriminate. They don't even recognize family."

"We were wondering why they kept circling the tree and wouldn't answer us. I was tripping because Dad was all bloody," the older boy said, wincing as he again looked at the dead bodies. The brothers, eyes tearing, embraced each other and cried.

Cade gave them a moment, then got their attention to add one last important detail. "The people on the news are saying the only way to stop the infected if they attack you is by destroying their brain. Hit 'em anywhere else and they just keep coming."

The whole exchange took just moments. Now undead were moaning all around them and it sounded as if they were drawing nearer.

Cade holstered his pistol, secured the ice axe to the bike's utility rack and quietly whispered to the two boys, "Follow me if you want to live."

The nerve wracking sounds coming from the large group of walkers, about a hundred yards away, were more than enough to convince the brothers to follow the stranger on the bike.

Chapter 5
Day 2 - Myrtle Beach, South Carolina

A woman's piercing scream came from downstairs. Sitting bolt upright, it took a minute for Brook to remember where she was. The clock read 8:37 A.M. Raven had shared the queen-sized bed with her. She was eleven now, but still a little small for her age. Being a heavy sleeper, she was slower to wake from the commotion downstairs in the kitchen.

Brook kept quiet, fearing an intruder had entered the house and attacked her mom. She stared at her daughter as she awoke with a start. She kept Raven quiet with a serious glare and a vertical finger to her lips. Stillness pervaded the house. She strained to hear anything more. Brook thought, *Dad must still be in bed, how could anyone sleep through that?*

*****

Brook's dad was an emergency room physician at Grand Strand Regional Hospital. Yesterday evening about 9:00 P.M. he was bitten by a patient. The feverish, hallucinating man bit him as he was leaning over, probing with his stethoscope to listen to his heart. As the orderlies tried to restrain the combative dying man, the hospital's first confirmed pandemic victim also bit one of them.

Before her dad came home, one of the other ER doctors cleaned the bite wound, bandaged him up and administered a shot of antibiotics. He had gone to bed before everyone else the previous night. He had cramps and was burning up with a high fever. The superficial bite wound on his abdomen was the least of his worries;

he had a strong suspicion he was sick with the new flu pandemic. The man that had bitten him had shown identical symptoms to the ones he was suffering from. Keeping his distance just in case, he had said, "See you in the morning. I love you Brook and my little bird, Raven."

*****

The noises resumed downstairs. To Brook it sounded like someone was moving furniture around. She silently ushered her daughter into the adjoining bathroom and gingerly pulled the door shut.

On stocking feet, she crept along the upstairs hall to the closed door of her dad's study. He kept an antique Ithaca shotgun displayed in his office on the wall behind his desk.

She found the closed office door unlocked. As she entered, the familiar smell of Dad's personal quiet space greeted her: leather, tobacco and of course Old Spice aftershave. Happy memories of her childhood flooded her brain.

Everything was where she remembered it, a black leather swivel chair behind his big wooden desk, and two maroon red overstuffed leather pub chairs, one in each corner by the door. All types of artifacts filled every nook and cranny. Above the bronze wild bronco statue and world globe was Dad's prized over and under Ithaca shotgun. Its pale walnut stock gleamed and the light from the hall reflected in the ornate etchings on the blued metal.

Cade had introduced her briefly to the basic workings of a firearm. They practiced a small amount of target shooting every time they went camping together.

Brook retrieved the shotgun and opened the breech. As she suspected, it was unloaded. After quietly rummaging through a couple of drawers, she found some loose shells. Carefully, she loaded both chambers. Then she descended the steps slowly one at a time. Loaded shotgun in hand, she went to investigate the noises, pausing on the bottom step to listen.

What she heard reminded her of a big dog greedily wolfing down wet canned dog food. Gun poised at the ready and safety off, she said, "Mom, Dad... is that you? I've got Dad's shotgun, it's loaded."

She thought, *I've lost the advantage now if there is an intruder in the house.*

Just then a mournful, haunting moan came from the kitchen. The sound made her hair stand on end. She had an urge to flee but stood her ground between the kitchen and the dining room. Craning her head to the right, she could see the blood-splashed travertine tiles beyond the black granite island. It looked like a slaughterhouse floor. Making her way into the kitchen, she noticed that breakfast ingredients were on top of the island. Eggs were broken on the floor and a plastic gallon of milk rested on its side, most of the milk pooled on the floor.

A strong coppery odor hung in the air, overpowering her mom's potpourri. The sight, smell and volume of blood caused Brook to gag. She could see a foot twitching on the other side of the island. She willed herself to put one foot in front of the other and cautiously rounded the corner enough to see the backside of her dad, still in his pajamas, tending to her mom.

Letting the barrel drop, she approached the scene frantically, calling out, "Dad, what happened to Mom? Did you call 911 yet?"

He rose slowly, turning towards her. She expected to see pain and anguish. Instead she saw his pale, slack face, bloody teeth and expressionless glassy eyes staring her down.

Leveling the gun without conscious thought at what used to be her father, Brook backpedaled. He came for her with a clumsy but determined, steady pace.

She had a feeling someone was watching her. Brook glanced back towards the bottom of the stairway where Raven, eyes wide as saucers, watched the horrifying events unfold.

Raven screamed *"Grandpa!"* as he neared the business end of his own shotgun.

Returning her attention to the advancing ghoul, Brook made the split second decision that saved their lives. She aimed for center mass, just as Cade had taught her. Brook pulled the trigger. The boom was deafening in the small hallway and the buck of the big gun caused her to fall back; the barrel rose and the buckshot blasted the creature in the neck and underneath the chin. Jaw bone and teeth disintegrated and its head whipped backward, impacting between the shoulder blades before tearing free, falling and rolling out of sight under the table. For a brief moment her dad's body trembled, and then with a slow motion tilting movement like a felled tree, the headless body smacked onto the tile floor like an unconscious boxer hitting the canvas.

Brook rushed around the island. What she saw sickened her. There was barely enough of her mom's neck left to feel for a pulse. Brook's training as a nurse dictated she check anyway. Putting the shotgun aside, she checked a wrist and found no pulse.

She fell to her knees next to her mom, crying uncontrollably. After allowing herself a moment of mourning Brook pulled herself together, grabbed the phone and called 911. She got a recording saying all circuits were busy. She tried repeatedly, never getting anything but the same recording.

Brook bolted from the house with her daughter in tow and together they went next door.

Chapter 6
Day 2 - Southeast Portland

The boys were silent as they followed the man. All three were beginning to sweat. It was July, so in the midmorning sun it was already 75 degrees and probably would reach 85 by noon.

Cade took a different route back to his house in case the dead had followed him. When the three were a block east of the house, they heard walkers well before they saw them. There were two: a female with a blood saturated cotton sundress pasted to her body, and a male minus most of his face. He wore a Pabst Blue Ribbon beer shirt, cargo shorts and only one flip flop which slapped the pavement as he walked.

Cade thought, *Probably a couple of Reed college students on summer break. Looks like school's out forever.*

The three of them hunkered down and remained quiet.

Just as the undead pair passed by, Cade's neighbor Rawley came speeding down the street in his older model white Ford Bronco. Cade liked to kid him about the "O.J. Simpson" truck he drove. The Bronco skidded to a stop abruptly in front of the green house two lots down and across the street from Cade's. It looked like he had been on a supply run, as he was hurriedly taking bags and boxes up his stairs and into the house.

Their attention aroused, the two infected college kids about faced and set course for Rawley. Bone chilling moans and the slapping of the frat boy's lone flip flop on the street signaled their approach.

Finished with his task, Rawley jumped into the still running SUV, cut a wide U-turn in the street and careened past the two, barely missing them. This again influenced their direction of travel and they clumsily about faced and followed the white Bronco.

*****

Rawley's house backed up to an alley and it was where he usually parked his truck. Cade guessed that was his destination.

The three-minute distraction allowed the trio to stealthily slip back into the alley from the east and proceed to the rear of Cade's home. They avoided detection and knelt in the thigh high grass near the back fence. After making sure all was clear, Cade helped the boys, one at a time, scale up and over the barrier. Next, he vaulted it with ease and double checked to make sure they were alone in the enclosed backyard. The yard was clear and the back door was still locked. Nothing seemed disturbed and the house was silent as they entered the kitchen.

They lived in a brown, two-story Craftsman style home with a two car garage; the driveway sloped down about thirty feet to the street. Next to the garage a padlocked wooden gate the same height as the rest of the fence opened into the backyard. The front door was sturdily constructed from solid oak. The back door led into a sun porch followed by another dead bolted door leading into the kitchen.

When everyone was in, Cade closed and locked the outer door. He had installed an extra dead bolt for added security. It wouldn't stop a determined intruder but it would slow them down.

Once inside, the boys relaxed a little. They jumped at the offer of something to eat.

While he prepared some peanut butter and jelly sandwiches, he introduced himself to the older boy. "My name is Cade."

With a furtive glance the bigger boy curtly replied, "Leo."

"And your brother's name?"

"His name is Isaac; he goes by Ike."

Ike had taken a walk around the family room while Cade and Leo talked. When he returned to the kitchen he asked, "Who is the little girl and lady in the pictures above the fireplace?"

Not wanting to go over it in detail, Cade simply said, "My wife and daughter."

Leo continued the interrogation. "Where are they now?"

26

"They're in South Carolina visiting my wife's parents."

"Why didn't you go with them?" Ike asked.

"I have a lot of projects that need finishing around here."

Abruptly ending the conversation Cade picked up the remote control and turned on the television. When the LCD flat screen came to life, the silent images of carnage and looting said more than words. They watched the muted television until the scene changed to the Oval Office of the White House and the President strode in and sat down in his plush chair. This was orchestrated to put the American people at ease. Seeing the man in his comfortable office as opposed to him standing and reading from his ever-present teleprompter was supposed to have a psychologically calming effect. To Cade it did the opposite. He couldn't put a finger on it but something didn't feel right about the scenario.

Cade turned up the volume in time to hear the anchor introduce President Bernard Odero. The President started off by telling the television audience he had been forced to declare martial law in Washington D.C. It was the first city to see signs of the infectious disease. Other areas of the country were also affected by the contagion. Los Angeles, San Francisco/Oakland and San Diego were the hardest hit on the West Coast. He recited a litany of Midwest cities including his hometown of Chicago. The entire Eastern Seaboard of the United States, Florida on up to Maine, was battling the epidemic as well. Air, maritime and rail travel had been canceled until further notice. High-speed transportation had initially led to the disease's prolific spread, while the localized pattern of outbreak seemed to start in the hospitals and radiate outward into the communities. President Odero emphasized that all resources were being utilized to determine the cause of the outbreak and find a cure.

While the President spoke, the crawl on the bottom of the television screen displayed a list of the countries already affected. The list was not short.

President Bernard Odero finished his speech by imploring the American people to remain home and stay strong; he promised the United States Government would not fail them.

Cade noted the absence of any mention of God at the end of Odero's speech. Being politically correct to the nth degree, it was par for the course for the President. Cade knew this would be the

27

"perfect crisis" that Odero's advisors would not let "go to waste" as some in the President's administration were fond of saying. Since the 9/11 attacks the sitting politicians on both sides of the aisle made every attempt to give themselves more power and the people less freedom. An event like this was sure to permit them free reign to make any constitutional changes they deemed necessary. As far as martial law in Portland was concerned, he was sure it loomed on the horizon.

Cade was baffled by the fact that the President was still in the District of Columbia at all. It also astonished him at how the most protected city in the world could fall so fast to the walking dead. One word quickly came to mind: "Rome."

After the President finished his somber speech, a White House pool reporter's head filled the screen and indicated that the President and his family would be moved to a secure and undisclosed location until the "unknown threats facing our nation were dealt with." The reporter's next piece addressed immigration and borders. Apparently, it took a pandemic of biblical proportions for the U.S. President to finally grow some balls and seal the southern border with Mexico. Between San Diego and Tijuana at the border checkpoint, hundreds of people on both sides had been attacked by the cannibalistic infected, resulting in upwards of three hundred deaths and counting. The capital, Mexico City, was a blood bath. The violence inflicted on the population by the infected made the Mexican drug war pale in comparison.

All day long the talking heads on every news channel were reporting about a deadly virulent new strain of flu that had not been encountered before. The Fox news anchor said a full-blown pandemic was rolling across the nation. Anyone that was bitten by a carrier also became infected. Death followed, sometimes quickly. Sometimes it took hours, but the main thing they stressed was that after succumbing to the infection, the newly dead would re-animate and attack any living thing they saw. The infection made the afflicted patient feverish, hallucinate and violence prone. Unconfirmed reports suggested a few cases had even ended in homicidal violence and then escalated to cannibalism. The anchorman finished by adding, as Cade had already discovered first hand, that the only way to kill them was to destroy their brain.

Cannibalism. The word alone made the hairs on the back of Cade's neck stand on end, especially after what had happened at Ted's house. Cade turned the TV off and went upstairs to the office to retrieve his phone; he passed the wall covered with photos of his family in good times: skiing, camping, holidays and school milestones. Cade felt a lump forming in his throat. His eyes lingered on the photo of the three of them all bundled up on Mount Hood, enjoying a family ski outing. Raven and Brook's smiling faces seared into his memory. He made up his mind at that moment; it was time to leave Portland and go locate his family.

Chapter 7
Day 2 - Southeast Portland

Since the outbreak started, cellular service had been nearly non-existent, and the DSL and land line phone was down and worthless. With a determined set of the jaw, Cade grabbed his phone and punched in the numbers to Brook's cell. A busy signal droned on in his ear. Taking a look at the phone's display, he was not surprised to see that there were no new voice mails or text messages. On a whim he tried again to call Brook on her cell. He was relieved to finally at least get her voice mail; he left her a brief disjointed message.

"This is Cade. I am worried about your safety. How is your Dad? He may be infected. Be careful. There is a serious contagion on the loose. It is transferred by saliva contact. The infected seem to go comatose or die and reawaken prone to violence. If anything happens there, if you see any of the infected... leave immediately and get to Fort Bragg and contact Mike Desantos. Call or text me when you get service. I love you two. Give Raven a hug for me, Daddy loves you. Bye."

Cade had no way of knowing if Brook would be able to access her voice mail or if his message would reach her at all. The instructors at Fort Benning always expected their pupils to have a backup plan. For redundancy's sake he also composed a lengthy text message.

I haven't heard from you and I couldn't get through to your mom and dad's phone... busy signal only? Be careful! There's definitely a pandemic! Get to Fort Bragg ASAP and contact Captain Mike Desantos 910-555-5555. He knows me from the Sandbox. Just refer to me as "Wyatt." Desantos is a good man and in the loop. At all costs stress the need to contact him or send him a message if they fail to allow you a face-to-face meeting. He will let you inside the wire. Love Cade.

Wyatt was Cade's nickname in the teams, the name derived from his prowess with a pistol. During training he held top score on many of the shooting drills. He also more than lived up to the name in combat.

All operators were given their nickname by their peers. Mike had been a member since the early days; his name came from the amount of time he had spent behind enemy lines in "Indian" country, so they started calling him "Cowboy."

Mike was Cade's commander and team leader in the 1st Special Forces Operational Detachment-Delta, or Delta Force for short. During the last deployment in Afghanistan they had seen a lot of combat together, and trusted each other with their lives.

During one particularly intense engagement they were about to be overrun by a much larger force of insurgents and Taliban. They had been forced to call in "danger close" artillery fire, and the rounds impacted all around and nearly on top of their position. A-10 Thunderbolts, heavily armored, slow moving, ground attack jets, the ground soldier's best friend, rolled in time after time making gun runs. The nose-mounted Vulcan cannons spit lead, decimating scores of enemy in the process. In the middle of the fighting, each man had vowed that should either one of them die the survivor would look after the other's family.

Mike Desantos's phone went to voice mail after the first ring. Cade left a concise message detailing his wife's and daughter's situation and asked him to be on the lookout for them.

Chapter 8
Day 2 - Myrtle Beach, South Carolina

Harrison and Peggy Mortenson had lived next to Brook's childhood home in the subdivision since 1960. They were nonstop news junkies and had been up most of the night, witnessing the contagion spread worldwide.

It was now apparent to Brook why her dad had committed the unspeakable act upon her mother. She also feared for her brother and the other workers still at the hospital.

"My phone has been acting up and I haven't heard from my husband since yesterday. This is the first I've heard about the contagion that's going around," Brook said to Peggy worriedly.

Harrison interjected and told Brook about how the infection occurred and what happened as a result. He added as an afterthought, "The President has issued a declaration of martial law. We are in a world of hurt."

Armed with this new information, Brook came to the realization that nobody would be coming to investigate what had just happened at her parents' house, and she surmised the coroner wouldn't be coming for the bodies either.

She turned to Raven. "I have to go back and get my phone so I can try to get ahold of your dad. I want you to come with me."

Shaking her head vigorously from side to side, Raven said, "No way Mom." She bit her bottom lip nervously. "Please don't make me." She wouldn't budge, and wanted no part of going back to Grandma's house.

Considering the horrors she had witnessed there minutes ago, Brook didn't force the issue. She reluctantly left her daughter with the Mortensons and went back to her childhood home one last time.

The door was ajar and the house smelled like gunpowder and death. Moving slowly into the kitchen, she could see her mom's feet clad in the pink slippers she had given her last Christmas. Out of the corner of her eye Brook detected movement. She looked closer; her mom's foot jerked.

Brook crept around the island and retrieved the shotgun from the bench in the breakfast nook. The ghoul sensed her arrival. The bloody remains that was once her loving mom flopped over onto its stomach and proceeded to crawl towards her, bodily fluids leaving a slick trail along the floor. Her undead mom slowly pursued her into the living room, leaving her no choice.

Remembering what Harrison had told her earlier, she aimed directly for the head. Brook closed her eyes for a second, said a little prayer and thought, *It's not you anymore, Mom. I love you and I'm sorry I have to do this.*

She pulled the trigger and the shotgun roared. The second random shell she had inserted happened to be a slug; the round ruptured her mom's head, peppering the hallway with brain matter, hair and bone fragments. She started sobbing as the realization that both of her parents were now dead suddenly hit her like a ton of bricks. She still had her daughter, that much she knew. She sent silent prayers out to her husband Cade, whom she missed terribly.

Brook ran up the stairs two at a time and went into her old room. Her phone was in her carry-on, where it had been since she last talked to Cade. Bag in hand, she went downstairs heading for the door.

Raven had run from the neighbors' house when she heard the shotgun report and was tentatively peering into the open front door when Brook descended the stairs. At the first sight of her mom, Raven ran and jumped into her arms. Brook sat on the porch swing comforting Raven; she held her and stroked her hair for a few minutes. Then she sent Raven back to the Mortensons' and watched to be sure she made it safely.

It took a few seconds of rooting around in her bag, but she finally found her phone and powered it on. It chimed several times letting her know she had missed calls and there were messages waiting for her. She sat on the porch reading the text message from Cade. Her head started spinning at the thought of what was happening everywhere else in the world. The voicemail from Cade drove the severity of their situation home; the tone of his voice on the message said it all. She would surely heed his advice because when it came to questions about their family's security, she never questioned his wisdom. Brook thought, *As soon as we get the Cadillac loaded up we'd better set out for Fort Bragg.*

She stood and went back into the house. Standing in the kitchen, Brook stared at her dad's lifeless form. She heard his voice in her head. *"Brooklyn, you get going now, take Raven and get to safety."* Of course it was only her subconscious talking, but she took it to heart.

Brook called her brother Carl. She tried both his cell and the hospital land line but had no luck reaching him. Next, she dialed Cade's cell and listened to it ring. After the third ring he picked up.

Chapter 9
Day 2 - Southeast Portland

While the kids ate, Cade closed all of the blinds and double checked the windows and doors, making sure all were locked. The undead didn't know they were in the house and Cade wanted to keep it that way.

Cade once again turned his attention to the local news. Two anchors were mourning their fellow reporter's demise that had been broadcast on live television the day before. Thankfully they refrained from showing the bloody spectacle again.

President Odero put on the full court press and declared martial law nationwide. FEMA issued recommendations that doomed millions. They urged the United States population to stay home and tend to their sick and wounded. The most disturbing information that Cade had to process was a graphic simulating the nationwide spread of the infection. It revealed an ever expanding zone indicated in red, which radiated inland from the Eastern Seaboard and spread north from Mexico. Despite the new border crackdown, the entire state of California was awash in red. The South and Southwest looked less impacted and the Northwest and Central Rockies weren't hit as hard... yet. The next graphic was unfathomable. A fast spreading, time lapsed representation of the contagion's impact worldwide filled the screen. There were very few locations on Earth not ravaged during the first two days of the global outbreak. As he watched the news, he had no clue that a thousand miles away his in-laws were dying.

Cade had no immediate family in Portland; both of his parents had died years ago. Chuck and Madeline were very close and had been married for fifty-five years when they both suddenly died of natural causes barely a month apart. Chuck passed first. He died peacefully in his sleep. Madeline was devastated and died of natural causes--probably of a broken heart--twenty-eight days later. Cade inherited the house he grew up in.

His parents had been happily married for twenty-seven years before Cade came along. He was not in their plans, but he was the best thing that had ever happened to them. Their proudest moment was when Cade joined the army at the age of twenty: Eleven Bravo. Light infantry was his MOS (Military Occupational Specialty) when he enlisted. He excelled during basic training and loved service life so much that he went through Ranger school, served with the 75th Ranger Regiment and then later went on to Special Forces training at Fort Benning, Georgia.

Mike Desantos recruited Cade for the Delta Force. For the next couple of years he had some top-secret missions where he found himself "down range," the soldier's term for being on the receiving end of enemy fire. Cade gave better than he got.

When he met Brook, it was love at first sight. She was a nurse near Fort Lewis when he was stationed there with the 1st Special Forces Group. It was 1999. They were soon married and Raven was born shortly thereafter.

Being an operator was his life, and when those nineteen shit bags dropped the Twin Towers it became a crusade. He believed in the war against terror so wholeheartedly that he had "INFIDEL" tattooed in Old English lettering across his back.

Cade did everything his superiors asked of him, sacrificing anniversaries, birthdays, he even missed Raven's first words and steps while he was hunting terrorists.

Soon after the new President took office and the crusade had lost its luster for the American people, Cade decided to hang up his spurs. It was a slap in the face to all of the people in uniform fighting for their country when the President and his new administration decreed that terrorist acts be called "man-made catastrophes." It was the final straw for Cade when the White House staff started omitting the word "terrorist" in official communications.

Choosing to leave his unit and not re-up was the hardest decision Cade had ever made. A lot of career shooters were also taking this route and then going to work for Blackwater or Triple Canopy, providing private security in the Sandbox.

Cade chose instead to immerse himself in family life.

Chapter 10
Day 2 - Southeast Portland

Cade's phone vibrated in his pocket. He extracted it and, seeing Brook's name and number on the display, he answered it immediately. Sobbing on the other end of the line was indeed his wife Brook. She began recounting everything that had happened to her in the last twenty minutes. Towards the end of her story, Cade cut her off and asked, "If my memory serves me, your parents live on a cul-de-sac, right?"

"Yes," she replied. "So?"

Not knowing how long he would have a signal, he told Brook to just listen. "It's a good thing they do. If Myrtle Beach is anything like Portland those things will be all over the surface streets. Get as many shells for the shotgun as possible. Grab some food and water from the house and take the Escalade and get Raven and yourself to Bragg. Stay away from big public places, especially hospitals or triage centers. The National Guard and FEMA will try to limit your travel. If they give you any problems tell them where you are going and whom you seek. Explain your relationship with me as a last resort. Remember to go around popular major routes. Do not pick up anybody, and give Rave a hug for me. I'll meet up with you at Bragg. See you soon, I love you."

"Finished yet?" Brook said jokingly.

"Just the pertinent facts, ma'am!" he fired back. Then all business aside, voice wavering, Cade said, "You guys be careful, and I really do mean it, I love you. See you soon."

Just then the connection was lost and replaced with the hiss of static.

There had been no time and no reason to tell Brook about Ted and Lisa, their neighbors from around the block. She had enough on her plate and Cade didn't want to muddy the waters any further.

*****

Brook was sitting on the neighbors' sofa and taking this all in when her brother skidded to a stop outside. He left his car running and sprinted into his parents' home.

By the time Brook walked out onto the lawn Carl had already been inside and seen his parents; he was on hands and knees hurling in the grass. When Carl finally stopped and wiped a trembling hand across his mouth, they met each other's gaze. His eyes were bloodshot and he looked exhausted. He looked at the shotgun Brook held and said, "I'm sorry you had to do it, Sis. Before I saw Mom and Dad in there I thought I could never convince you what went on at the hospital. It was a hell house. I'll never forget last night." Breathing in deeply, he continued. "Earlier this morning I had a moment of clarity and remembered the bite that Dad got. I tried to call here; I only got a recording. Shortly after, people in the Emergency Room started screaming." Carl paused, wiping his nose with his shirt sleeve. "I hid in a closet for over three hours until the wailing stopped. I finally decided to run for it. By then, everyone on the wing was either dead or a walking corpse. I drove here as fast as I could," he gasped, eyes red-rimmed and teary.

As Raven joined them, Brook hugged her little girl and big brother close to her.

Chapter 11
Day 2 - Southeast Portland

Ike and Leo were still mesmerized by the images on TV; they couldn't turn it off. It was like being in a car going by a fatal wreck and seeing the telltale yellow tarp, you are compelled to steal a look. Such was the draw here. They aired the Pioneer Square footage yet again, the attack at the hospital and a reporter getting ambushed by a mob of undead at an outdoor triage center. The international footage was few and far between. What they did show mirrored the horrors they faced here in the United States. As time wore on governments worldwide began to hide the extent of the outbreak. Even FEMA started a looping video message on all of the channels warning of the contagion and imploring people to shelter in place.

Leo and Ike watched the news for an hour and tried to piece together what had happened to their parents.

Their mom had been a janitor in a high-rise office building downtown, working the swing shift. She must have gotten infected downtown or at her job, turned undead sometime after she arrived home and attacked their dad when he came downstairs all dressed up for church. Unfortunately they would never really know what happened. They were very fortunate Leo had gotten them out of their house alive, and truly blessed that Cade came along when he did.

Cade had talked Leo and Ike out of going home to bury their parents. It was a noble thing to do but with all of the undead walking the streets, it wouldn't be safe.

Leo told Cade that most of their extended family lived in Georgia and Louisiana. Cade suggested they go with him and they could look for their family members together. The brothers had no other family in Portland so there was little hesitation. Leo made the executive decision for himself and his brother. "We will go, but can you teach us to shoot a gun so we can defend ourselves?"

After giving it some thought, Cade answered, "I'll teach you guys the safety part first. If you can grasp that... then, yes."

The silver Toyota Sequoia should serve them well on their cross country trek. With the third row seat folded out of the way, there was plenty of room for the supplies they intended on taking.

Chapter 12
Day 2 - Southeast Portland

Rawley had himself quite a fan club. From his vantage point in Raven's bedroom on the second floor, Cade could see at least twenty walkers around the front and sides of his neighbor's house across the street. One of the putrid creatures was on the porch pawing at the door.

It looked like Rawley had shored up his big picture window. The bottom of the sofa was visible through the glass. Fortunately the narrow basement windows were too small for the ghouls to fit through, and the windows on the sides of the house were well above ground level.

Cade couldn't remember what Rawley's backyard looked like, even though he'd been to a few barbecues there. He did remember that Rawley's hickory smoked beef ribs were awesome.

Over the years he had proven to be a pretty nice fellow. He played guitar and looked the part. His long hair was dyed black and he had full sleeve tattoos on both arms. Rawley occasionally toured with a rock band, which meant that a lot of different girls came and went from his house. Cade knew these were the perks of the lifestyle, and as far as he knew Rawley didn't have an exclusive woman living with him.

It looked as if his plan of circling the wagons with his guitar and supplies wasn't going to work. Rawley had been a little careless and let the walkers see him taking things in the front door.

The undead's senses didn't seem that adversely affected. Their movement suffered a little and their speed was usually about halved, but some were faster and some were slower.

The lone zombie on the porch had lost its infatuation with the door and started banging on the big plate window. The glass shattered with a loud report, drawing the attention of other walkers in the vicinity.

What happened next was the last thing Cade had anticipated. The front door opened and Rawley emerged with an SKS assault rifle, pregnant with a fifty round drum magazine. It was the type of rifle the two bank robbers used to outgun the police in North Hollywood in the early nineties. Rawley dispatched the one on his porch with two well-placed shots to the head. Flesh and brain matter splattered his welcome mat. Carefully aimed bullets cut down more walkers on the bottom stairs leading to the porch.

Cade had never seen Rawley mad before. Now he was channeling Rambo.

Cade left his perch at the bedroom window, went into the office and punched his PIN on the gun safe's keypad. He pulled out his Colt M4 and four loaded thirty round magazines. It was a civilian model kitted out just like the personal weapon he used on deployment. Uncle Sam kept the fully automatic M4 when Cade left the teams.

Returning to the room that overlooked the front of the house, by feel he seated a magazine, pulled the charging handle and switched the selector to fire. Bracing the rifle against his shoulder he practiced steady controlled fire and made his contribution to the body count.

At first Rawley looked up at him with a bewildered look, but recognition dawned on his face and with renewed determination he kept on shooting.

Ike and Leo joined Cade in the front bedroom upstairs and marveled at the shooting display. It was not planned but Cade and Rawley had the undead in a withering crossfire.

Cade yelled above the din at the two brothers. "Ike, go downstairs, load the truck in the garage with all of the canned food, and then throw in all of the dry stuff that will fit."

Gesturing towards the open door in the hall he said "Leo, go into the office over there and take all of the ammo and magazines from the safe and throw them in this," tossing a long black bag his way. "Do you know what a magazine looks like?"

"It's the square thing that fits in the gun, right?"

"You got it. When everything is in the bag, have Ike help you put it in the Sequoia," Cade said.

The two boys sprinted down the stairs. Ike stopped near the front door as a shadow moved past the living room window. Curiosity got the best of him. He reached up and pried opened the louvered wooden slats a half an inch. A gaunt gray face with milky eyes peered back at him.

Ike bolted back upstairs out of breath exclaiming, "The walkers are on the front porch now. I looked out the kitchen window and it looks like the backyard is still clear if we need to leave that way."

Leo added, "The sound of the shooting sure is attracting a lot more of them."

Having concluded the house wouldn't be safe for much longer, Cade told the two boys to go downstairs, get in the truck and be ready to go.

Rawley had culled most of the undead that had his house under siege. At least fifteen of the corpses were piled around the porch. The dead girl in the bloody sundress was splayed out exposing herself in an unflattering way. She faced downstairs head first and her dress was pulled up around the top of her torso. Flip flop boy in the PBR shirt had been shot through the eye socket and now lay on the pile of corpses as well.

During a lull in the gunfire, Cade yelled loud enough so Rawley could hear him. "We are coming out in three minutes and are going to create a diversion for you!" He then entered the garage, drew his Gerber knife and cut two four-foot lengths off of the coiled garden hose hanging on the wall. "God Damn!" Cade muttered angrily to himself as he remembered he had left the ice axe strapped to his bike in the alley; it would have to stay behind. He had the two Glocks on his person. He stowed the M4 carbine up front in the truck, safety on, with the stock fully collapsed.

Cade put a second long black canvas bag containing his other rifle and tactical gear in the back of his truck. A box marked Camping Gear held the headlamps, a pair of two-way radios, Bushnell armored binoculars and a camp stove. Next went the tent and three sleeping bags which they tossed unceremoniously into the back of the truck. Lastly he threw two empty five gallon potable water containers on top of everything and closed the door.

Peering through the small glass windows lining the top of the garage door, he saw that the bulk of the remaining walkers were now on his porch and trampling the front yard. A very large ghoul was trudging up the driveway. A pair of walkers leaned on the front window and fell into the living room riding a wave of shattered glass. The smell of death permeated his home.

Cade climbed into the truck and turned the key in the ignition. The V8 rumbled to life. He punched the remote button that started the garage door's plodding upward movement. Achingly slow, it revealed the sunny outside and the giant rotting roadblock standing five feet away. He was missing most of his left arm. With each step the stub twitched like a dog's cropped tail. Along with the arm, most of the flesh was missing from one leg leaving the white femur and kneecap exposed, all the while lending to his slow gait.

At first sight of the truck and its occupants, the one armed gargantuan started moaning excitedly, alerting the other walkers of his find.

The ghouls swarmed inside the house through the broken front window, spilled into the garage and began banging on the back of the SUV.

"Go, go, go….!" Ike screamed hysterically from the back seat of the Sequoia, staring eye to eye with Cade's dead next door neighbor, Dave. Judging from his condition, he wasn't here to borrow tools.

The instant the door was fully opened, Cade gunned the truck forward. Several undead now flanked the driveway. They pawed at the closed side windows as the three ton truck sucked the muscular one armed ghoul under the front skid guard; its skull popped like an overripe melon as a rear wheel rolled over it.

Cognizant of the ghoul-filled garage behind them, he stopped the SUV momentarily to survey the scene across the street. There was no sign of Rawley.

Chapter 13
Day 2 - Southeast Portland

The walkers were converging on them from both directions. From the west came the largest group he had seen yet. Cade noticed that the more walkers there were, the faster they seemed to move.

Easing out onto the road fronting his house he paused to steal a last glance at the home he grew up in. He said a silent goodbye, unsure he would ever see it again.

He planned to creep slowly east up the street and try to get as many of the dead to follow them as he could. At this slow of a pace the walkers were crowding around trying to get into the truck. The ones too slow to get out of the path of the truck ended up fleshy speed bumps. The Sequoia's windows were getting smeared with gore from the zombies' attempts to get at them.

In the rear view mirror Cade noticed flashing headlights. It was Rawley in the Bronco trying to get his attention. He sped up to get a safe distance from the walkers, then pulled over to the right on the shoulder and waited.

Rawley opened his window as he pulled up next to the Sequoia.

"Man, those fucks were getting thick out there. Your house was on the verge of getting overrun also," he commented cheerfully.

"A couple of them broke my front window right as we were finishing loading up the gear. Persistent bastards, aren't they?" Cade added.

"Persistent is an understatement. I was hoping to ride this out at home. You're right, those fucks are very determined. We're lucky, it looks like we both got out of there just in the nick of time. Hey, I need to thank you for stepping in when you did. Where the hell did they all come from anyway?" asked Rawley.

"The two that saw you unloading supplies alerted the others in the area when they started that fucking moaning."

"I had no idea it was that bad, but I wanted to get some groceries just in case," Rawley said.

"What store was open?" Cade queried him.

"The only one I found was the Mini Mart on Holgate. I had to use my credit card because every marked price was jacked up twentyfold. I had no beer in my house either, so I got their last case. That little bit of stuff ran me four hundred dollars. The beer alone was half of the cost. No worries though, if I ever see another credit card statement I'll be amazed. Shit's changed forever, man."

Nodding his head in agreement Cade said, "You hit the nail on the head. I was hunkered down in my house since this all started. I have to confess though, I haven't been very neighborly lately. I had to kill Ted from around the block... he left me little choice."

An incredulous look adorning his face, Rawley asked what happened.

Sparing no detail, Cade told him about his first introduction to this new reality.

"Heavy shit, man. If I turn into one of those fuckers, please finish me quickly, will ya?" Rawley implored his neighbor with a deadly serious look thrown in for good measure.

Reaching into the center console Cade said, "Take this."

A two-way radio sailed through Rawley's open window.

"10-1 is the channel we will be on. We're heading southeast to find Brook and Raven. Along the way I hope to help these two find some family."

"Mind if I tag along?"

"We could use another set of eyes and ears. Just wondering, where did you learn to shoot like that?"

"I come from a family of hunters. I've been hunting since I was six or seven. I like to shoot recreationally as well."

"And the SKS..."

"Oh, this little guy," he said, affectionately patting the rifle on the seat next to him. "I bought it at a gun show quite some time ago. Hell of a fun weapon to shoot!"

Cade smirked. "Yeah I could tell."

They had been sitting on the side of the road for a few moments before Leo interrupted.

"There are some of those dead thingies coming."

Cade saw the walkers. They were far enough away that they weren't a threat, but there was also a small compact car with those stupid blinding blue headlights closing very fast from the same direction.

Rawley attempted to wave the car around but the driver locked the brakes and slewed the gaudy Nissan to a sudden stop in front of the two SUVs.

The neon-green import sported a rear wing that belonged on a top fuel dragster. Low-rider was an understatement. The car sat so low it nearly scraped the pavement. The car's occupants glared at them. The passenger in the front seat was a Hispanic male wearing black wraparound sunglasses. A bloody do rag covered his head, gang banger style. Sitting in the rear passenger side of the four door Maxima was an Eminem-wannabe white kid with bad acne; he was brandishing a chrome semi-automatic pistol. The front seat passenger flashed an Ingram Mac-10 machine pistol. He had a shit-eating grin on his face and his gold grill glinted in the sun. The driver was mostly obscured from view.

Not impressed, Rawley and Cade produced their own guns. A bright crimson beam emanated from the SKS and settled on Slim Shady's neck. Cade leveled his M4, safety off, hand on the fore-grip and steadied the barrel next to his side mirror while keeping the door between him and the gang bangers.

Leo stared straight ahead, slowly sinking into the front passenger seat.

"Smoke the banger fucks," Ike said from the back seat.

"They may leave us no choice, Ike," Cade replied in a hushed voice without removing his eyes from the carjackers.

"Mind your own business, bro, and get your head down," Leo ordered, playing the parent role.

The banger in the front seat spoke up proudly. "We're MS13, fool, and we takin' those trucks, motherfuckers…"

Cade didn't let him finish. "Looks like we're in disagreement here fellas! Move the car and we go our separate ways… no conditions. I'll count to three. One…"

He only made it to one before the dumbass in the front seat started to swing the muzzle of the machine pistol in Cade's direction.

Their true intentions made known, Cade caressed the trigger on his carbine. The .223 caliber round went through the banger's gold grill, demolishing every tooth in his mouth and severing his carotid artery before exiting below his right ear. He wore a surprised look on his toothless mug as he voided his bowels and slumped forward, dying. The impact spun his shades from his face and the bloody bandana flew off, revealing a festering bite wound on his clean shaven dome.

Simultaneously Rawley's perfectly placed three round burst impacted right where the laser was aimed, erasing the Eminem-wannabe's acne addled face.

In the split second that followed, the panicked driver of the low-rider popped the clutch and mashed the accelerator to the firewall. The little sports car fishtailed and sped away out of control. The horrible sound of tearing metal and breaking glass followed as he wrapped it around a telephone pole fifty yards down the street. The pole shuddered and swayed but didn't fall.

The undead were only a hundred feet away and steadily approaching, drawn by the accident and gunfire.

Cade and Rawley drove towards the crumpled Maxima. The destroyed car now steadily leaked water and antifreeze.

After slowly rolling to a stop next to the mangled car, Cade put the Sequoia into park and got out. While he was looking inside the wreck, another car stopped.

"Oh my God, is everything OK?" asked a frantic, middle-aged lady. Her car was loaded to the roof with what appeared to be all of her worldly belongings.

"It is now," Cade said, giving her a tip of his ball cap.

Eyeballing the two pistols on his person and the big machine gun in his hand, she stammered "I, I, I'll call the police!" as she sped away with the phone to her ear, apparently calling 911.

Good luck with that, Cade thought grimly.

While they were interacting with the Good Samaritan, the toothless passenger reanimated and began fighting the airbag to get at Cade.

The driver, while still alive, was just coming to the realization that his legs were crushed and his midsection was stuck behind the steering wheel. Worst of all, he was within biting range of his undead homie.

Cade saw that the white boy in the backseat had been head shot by Rawley. He was the lucky one and would stay dead.

Pinned and helpless, the driver started screaming and calling out for his mom as the undead passenger bit his neck and tore away a mouthful of flesh and muscle. Blood sprayed everywhere while the attack continued.

Rawley asked Cade, "Aren't you going to put them out of their misery?"

"Not a chance in hell. Thankfully, some things are worse than death."

Chapter 14
Day 2 - Felony Flats, Outer Southeast Portland

The encounter with the hoodlums was an eye opener. Not only were the dead a threat but so were some of the living. Anarchy would be close on the heels of the breakdown of society. Most people had no idea there was only a thin veneer between their comfortable lives and the end of civilization as they knew it. It happened most recently during Hurricane Katrina in the South, and it was happening everywhere now. From now on it was a dog eat dog world. Cade really wasn't surprised that no one responded to the automatic weapons fire in a residential neighborhood. Cops and soldiers are people too. When the shit hits the fan, their families and loved ones go to the top of the list. This he understood all too well.

"Folks, we are now on our own. Shoot first and ask questions later!" Cade said loudly to anyone within earshot as he reloaded his rifle.

It was still morning. There was very little traffic but it was going the wrong way. Usually there would be a torrent of vehicles heading downtown to start the nine-to-five grind.

Cade made a conscious decision to travel the back roads while they were still close to Portland and then avoid altogether the bigger cities they would encounter later. Soon the surge out of town would exponentially increase and he wanted to be ahead of the curve. There was an old highway that paralleled I-84 along the Columbia River; it was the one they planned to travel.

Cade struck up a conversation with Leo. "I've seen you guys riding your bikes in the neighborhood. How long have you two lived there?" He was careful not to bring up their parents, considering what he had done to save the kids from their precarious perch in the tree house. Then Cade thought, *What the hell am I doing? Remember to keep things professional.*

"I guess since about third grade for me," Leo said.

Ike piped up from the back seat, "I was a baby when we moved in."

"How old are you guys now?"

"I'm nine." Ike said.

Leo exclaimed, "I'm seventeen and I just got my driver's license at the start of the summer."

Cutting their conversation short, Rawley's voice came over the two-way radio. "Come in. Hey, are you guys there?"

Cade grabbed his radio from the center console. "I hear you ,what's up?"

"I've been watching my rearview since we had to shoot up those assholes back there. Don't look now, but half of the Army is crawling up our ass."

The radio in Cade's hand beeped as Rawley let go of the transmit button. A convoy of noisy military vehicles overtook them at forty-five miles per hour. Both SUVs slowed and moved aside. They were still in the city but the thoroughfare was lightly travelled. There were two Humvees, three Bradley fighting vehicles, and four more Humvees bringing up the rear.

The longhaired Rawley caught icy glares from the sunglass wearing troopers riding shotgun in the trailing vehicles. He keyed his mic. "Where do you suppose they're going?"

"I don't want to be anywhere near where they're going... As far as I could tell they were in full battle rattle and frosty as hell. Also you don't just drive a Bradley Fighting Vehicle in an American city unless you plan on using it," Cade pointed out bleakly.

"What do you think they're going to be doing?" Ike persisted.

"With that many fully armed Bradleys, Humvees and a platoon of soldiers all heading towards the interstate ... my guess is they will be setting up roadblocks on the interstate *and* the bridges.

53

They've probably been ordered to stop travel between Oregon, Washington and Idaho," Cade answered.

"We better find a back road then," Leo said.

Cade called Rawley on the two-way. "I've been thinking, we should go out the old historic highway that runs along I-84, circumventing traffic and roadblocks until we get near Hood River."

Keying his mike Rawley answered, "I concur."

Chapter 15
Day 2 - Myrtle Beach, South Carolina

Brook helped Carl wrap their parents' bodies in their favorite comforters. They gently placed them side by side in the tin garden shed. They barely fit into the cramped space. Their parents deserved to be buried, but considering the dire circumstances it was the best they could do.

Raven looked on, a tear making a slow descent down her cheek as the padlock clicked shut. She bowed her head thinking to herself, *I just want to wake up from this nightmare, please.*

"Raven," Brook called out. "Grab your bag, we're leaving with Uncle Carl right now!"

Snapping out of her funk, Raven did as she was told.

Carl looted his late parents' pantry and loaded up the pearl white Cadillac Escalade. In Carl's opinion the Escalade was too luxurious to be used off road, but it would surely make travel easier. The gussied up four-by-four had more ground clearance and there was more interior space than his car.

The Mortensons were adamant about staying in their home. "We have a full pantry, a gun and the will to stay," Peggy said.

Brook and Carl both knew there would no persuading the couple. They said a tearful goodbye. Carl drove the Escalade, Brook rode in the front passenger seat armed with the loaded shotgun, and Raven was sitting in between them.

"We need at least one more shotgun for protection, plus more ammo for the Ithaca and a pistol if we can find one" Carl said to Brook. They had scavenged only eleven slugs and four shot shells for the Ithaca out of the drawer in the study.

It was still early so Carl decided to gamble and head for the interstate. They rounded the corner leaving the cul-de-sac and Brook let out an audible sigh. Smoke dominated the horizon from the multiple fires downtown. They left Myrtle Beach without a real plan except to somehow reunite with Cade.

They drove inland; the traffic at this hour was still light. Two Black Hawk helicopters, flanked by Apache gunships bristling with rockets under their stubby wings, roared overhead flying very low on a northern heading up the coast. If she had to venture a guess, Brook thought they must be heading to Fort Bragg. She knew those were the type of helicopters Cade used to ride in on the secretive missions Delta Force frequently undertook.

Carl was 45 years old, bald, divorced, overweight and a little out of shape. He was also a recovering alcoholic with a great wit and a jaded outlook on life. Being 6-foot-4, he struck an imposing figure. Around Raven, however, he was a big teddy bear. With Brook, Carl always played the big brother role; he was almost 10 years older than his little sister and overly protective. He had even vetted all of her boyfriends, going so far as to return to his old high school and spy on them without her knowledge. More than one of her suitors did not pass the "Carl" litmus test and were intimidated into finding someone else to date. Carl wasn't sold on Cade at first, but upon finding out that he had volunteered to go into harm's way for his country, his opinion instantly changed 180 degrees. The man was a great father to Raven, and Brook glowed in his presence. If there was anything he could do to help them find Cade, he was all in.

Chapter 16
Day 2 - Interstate 84, outside of Portland

The U.S. Army's moving screen served the two vehicle convoy well. Cade followed about a 1000 yards behind them, Rawley's vehicle close behind.

The Troutdale exit would take them to the old highway. Cade saw brake lights flash on up ahead as the military convoy came to a halt, presumably by a road block. A moment later as the Sequoia neared the stopped vehicles, the military convoy they had been tailing was waved through and pulled away.

There was an Oregon State Police Dodge Charger stopped to the left, partially blocking the road. The red and blue lights of the patrol car flashed hypnotically. The trooper wearing the trademark Smokey the Bear hat put up his gloved hand. Cade came to a stop, turned off the engine and handed his military identification to the trooper.

The trooper, eyes fixed on Cade, asked "What's your destination?"

Considering the trucks were loaded with his camping gear, Cade responded "We're headed to Trillium Lake to do some camping; if the sites are all full then we'll try Timothy Lake. My friend's driving the white Bronco behind me."

"Who are these kids travelling with you?"

"They're my neighbor kids, it's their first time camping."

"Haven't you been listening to the radio?" the trooper demanded.

"No we've been listening to CDs… why, what's up?"

"So… you are not aware that the State of Oregon is currently under a declaration of martial law and there have been deadly viral outbreaks in Portland?"

"I heard about some sick people but honestly, I had no idea martial law had been declared. We've been planning this trip for a while. This weekend worked the best for Ike and Leo's parents. They were going out of town on business and needed someone to watch these two anyway."

Ike and Leo gave each other the look only a sibling would understand; without words, it said they needed each other and had to stay strong to survive the loss of their parents. Both boys remained stoic during the trooper's questioning.

Cade finished by saying , "I figured no better time than now. Hopefully this contagion thing will blow over."

Glancing at the ID card the trooper looked at the three of them one at a time, pausing for a tick while locking eyes, then said, "I'm going to let you pass. Just remember to drive safe," then looking directly at the boys he added, "and be careful around the water, fellas." He glanced at Cade. "Wait here a moment while I speak with your friend."

The trooper continued down the line of vehicles that had begun to form behind Cade's Sequoia. Seeing as how the truck was full of guns and ammo, Cade couldn't wait to disengage from the officer and get moving. He tensely watched the trooper in his side mirror as he slowly walked towards Rawley's Bronco.

Rawley had patiently observed the stop unfold; he now removed his sunglasses as the trooper closed the distance with his truck.

The radio on the passenger seat came to life.

Quick and to the point Cade said, "We are going camping on Mount Hood at Timothy or Trillium Lake if he asks you," and then it went silent again.

Rawley provided his identification and received the same stock informative lecture, followed by the same questions from the officer. Because of his tattoos and long hair, his driver's license received more than a cursory inspection. Rawley informed the officer that he was going camping with the guys in the truck ahead of him, gesturing with his thumb towards the camping gear which fortunately was shielding his rifle from view. Rawley got his driver's license back and the trooper indicated he could follow Cade and the boys through the roadblock.

Cade waited as the trooper returned to the Sequoia. Behind him the drivers in the cars that were lining up started honking intermittently. The trooper reached in the window and handed the ID card back to Cade and then queried him about his service.

Downplaying his role, Cade said, "I did a tour in Iraq, nothing worthy of a medal. I was mostly in the Green Zone."

After a short pause he got a heartfelt "Thanks for your service, son," and with a tip of his stiff brimmed hat the older trooper exclaimed loudly enough to be heard over the honking, "you... and you!" pointing at the Sequoia and the Bronco, "carry on!" and waved them through. He then faced the unenviable task of telling the rest of the drivers in queue that I-84 was now closed.

Wasting no time, Cade started the Sequoia and hurriedly pulled away from the roadblock.

Rawley threw the trooper a quick smart ass salute as he rolled past him heading east away from the city of 1.2 million.

Chapter 17
Day 2 – Interstate 84 Roadblock

Trooper Gary England stood his ground as each person in front of him pled their case. His stature was imposing to most, and people usually listened to what he had to say. Today the people he was trying to reason with were attempting to flee the unknown carnage unfolding twenty miles to the west in Portland, Oregon. Bottom line, he was holding court with anxiety, panic and pandemonium.

An attractive young woman in denim shorts and a tank top shrilly dressed him down.

"You are not listening to me. My daughter is four years old and she is sitting in that car in the hot sun," she said while wildly stabbing her manicured nail at a black Mercedes.

"*And you, lady, are not hearing me.* I repeat, no one is getting through. The city is under forty-eight hour quarantine."

A balding middle-aged man and his wife started whining about the idiots in the city looting and rioting.

"I want your badge number!" the half-drunk wife bellowed. She obviously wasn't used to being told "no."

The trooper did his best to try and turn around the fifteen or so people who got out of their cars to "help" with the lobbying process.

Like a clap of thunder, the sound of approaching V-twin engines drowned out all conversation. Scores of bikes pulled up on both sides of the group of people trying to gain passage into the gorge.

Most of the outlaw bikers were flying their colors. Greasy leather jackets were emblazoned with the "Nomad Jester" patch. It had a devious looking jester wearing a floppy hat with round tassels on the end. Instead of a silly smile on its face it wore a devilish sneer; across its chest was an AK-47 held at port arms.

Trooper England, his hand on his Beretta, stared down the lead element of the pack.

One of the biggest bikers he had ever seen dismounted a black Harley. The behemoth extended the kickstand with his scuffed black leather boot. The red-bearded outlaw squared up with the trooper. He didn't offer his hand to the law let alone a modicum of respect.

"Just as I have been telling these fine citizens, the City of Portland is under quarantine for the next forty-eight hours." Hitching up his gun belt the trooper added, "You all need to turn around and go ho...."

Before Trooper Gary England could finish his sentence, a fifty caliber bullet traveling at 2800 feet per second entered just below his left eye socket. His head became a pink mist that covered the travelers around him with tiny pieces of vaporized brain, blood and pebble sized flecks of bone. Time seemed to stand still for the people clustered around the man. Then people gathered their wits and chaos broke out. The shrieking started with the drunk lady first. Most everyone made for their cars in an attempt to escape the menacing gang.

Three hundred yards away the former-Marine scout sniper turned outlaw biker put down his Barrett sniper rifle and high fived his buddy.

As if on cue, the rest of the gang attacked the innocent people with fists, knives and guns. Men were not spared. One biker decapitated the whiny middle-aged man with a machete. While his lifeblood pumped from the stump of his neck the assailants dragged his drunken wife away kicking and screaming. She was flex cuffed and thrown into a civilian Hummer2 driven by one of the biker's old ladies.

The massacre was swift and complete. They spared the mom that had been in the trooper's face, two teenage girls who had just witnessed their parent's murder and a twenty-something redhead hitchhiking with an elderly man. They were all trying to flee the madness in Portland and this is what they received in return.

Had he arrived two minutes sooner the man would have found himself in the middle of a massacre. While he watched helplessly two of the bikers held up the little girl. Even as she struggled valiantly the big red-bearded animal gutted her with his machete. Duncan hadn't witnessed anything like this since his first tour in Vietnam. The mom wailed on her hands and knees, cradling the remains of her little girl as the bikers laughed.

It took a three-point turn for him get the wide, long bed pickup pointing in the other direction on the narrow two lane road. Trying to literally put the scene in his rear view mirror, he raced east on the old scenic highway.

Chapter 18
Day 2 - Fort Bragg, North Carolina

The moment President Odero had called for nationwide martial law, secure smart phones rang and vibrated across the country as operators were mobilized to return to post. The Tier-One operators all had secure encrypted phones utilizing government satellites to keep everyone in constant contact.

Mike Desantos was on the phone with his base commander, Major Phillip Link, giving him a situation report.

"Sir, the call has been made; all of the active shooters have been ordered RTB. Half of our active Alpha Teams are in the 'Stan, and days away. Coronado is calling in all of their support personnel, SEAL Teams One and Ten are on deployment but most of the other teams have formed up and are on base. I just received word that the East Coast garrisons are doing call backs. SEAL Team Six is in Afghanistan hunting HVTs. We recently received a sit-rep from them, they want an exfil ASAP. Their last transmission indicated everyone in the Middle East is going to meet their seventy two virgins pretty soon. Almost all of the civilian communications are down. At least we have our satellite comms up and running for our operators."

Cutting his subordinate off Major Link said "Captain Desantos, I need to see you ASAP. I have a high priority mission for you."

"Right away sir, give me five mikes."

Captain Desantos walked across the base from the north entry to have a face-to-face with his commander. He was summoned in after knocking on the door to the air-conditioned communications room.

Captain Desantos saluted his superior and was greeted with the same, followed by an "At ease" coming from Major Link.

"What do you have for me sir?"

Straight and to the point, Link said, "POTUS (President of the United States) is incommunicado and has been since 03:00 EST."

Mike's face blanched at the news. "Last known location?" he asked.

"1600 Pennsylvania Avenue. Apparently he thought he would be safe there... ride it out with his family," the Major said, shaking his head. "All comms are down in the district. Our NSA bird sent back images of Marine One sitting on the south lawn. The walking dead are on the grounds and no living beings have been seen in the vicinity since communications ceased."

"What are the rules of engagement?"

"Shoot to kill any undead on sight no matter who they may be. POTUS and all VIPs must be rescued at all costs. If there are any casualties amongst them, then documentation is necessary. Take any credentials from the bodies and obtain DNA swabs and digital video to confirm their identity and condition. Protect you and your men at all costs," the Colonel said while patting the operator on the shoulder.

"I'll take two teams of six. Have the Night Stalkers been briefed?"

"Yes. They will be ready in thirty mikes. Two 160th SOAR Pave Hawks with Apache support." The Major paused and adjusted his black beret before saying, "It's bad out there... worse than any of our war gaming scenarios suggested. Watch your six, Cowboy."

The two men exchanged salutes.

The red phone on the commander's desk chirped. An MP made it very clear the perimeter needed fortification and he wanted to call McCord AFB to request that a Spectre gunship be brought on station. The Spectre was a close air support modified AC-130 with multiple weapons proven to be devastating against enemy forces on the ground.

"I'll make it happen, in the meantime keep me updated!" Major Link barked as he hung up.

*****

At SOCOM headquarters, Fort Bragg, North Carolina, MPs were checking identifications at the double gate in front of the compound. Cars and SUVs full of soldiers and family that usually lived off of base were lined up for blocks. The first priority of the guards would be to quarantine the injured and ensure none of the infected got inside.

Overnight, several hundred walkers had amassed around the perimeter having been attracted by the commotion and halide lights. The snipers in the guard towers had orders to confirm with thermal imaging if their targets were in fact walking dead before engaging them. The undead didn't have the same heat signature as the living. The newly turned did show up as almost normal for the first few minutes, therefore any questionable targets also required a visual identification.

Dawn broke and the day wore on as hundreds more of the infected streamed across the highway from the hospital and the surrounding businesses. Bodies of the infected were bulldozed into mass graves as fast as the snipers and tower guards could put them down.

Mike had checked his phone for personal messages. One was from his wife Annie, saying she was en route with their two girls. Annie was pregnant with Mike's first boy. Mike thought, *Only two more months of being the only male of the household.* Message number two was Cade. Mike listened intently, hung up and called each of the three gate houses. He left orders to look out for anyone fitting Brook's description as well as anyone that was with her. They were to let them in and contact Mike immediately. Cade's family was his family, as far as Mike was concerned.

*****

Private First Class Chillcut had his hands full checking identities and making sure the infected were kept outside of the wire. Things at the south entrance were getting hairy.

Back to back, staccato reports of automatic gunfire came from his left, and the third vehicle in line failed to move forward. Inside the car, one of the soldiers had turned and attacked the other occupants of the Ford Taurus wagon. The driver shrieked as her head was pulled towards the backseat, her undead husband's teeth sinking into the soft part of her neck ripping free a mouthful of flesh. He then turned his attention to the crying baby in the car seat. The baby's wailing intensified as the monster tried to wrest it from the car seat.

Seeing this happening through his thermal scope, the sniper in the nearest tower opened fire. The bullet entered the ghoul's head at the base of the neck, causing it to slump over the baby.

Having just bled out, the mom in the front seat reanimated and began banging on the driver's side window. Bursts of gunfire from the soldiers at the checkpoint killed her. The troops rushed to the car to check for survivors. The first to arrive at the vehicle's open window could hear muffled cries escaping from under the dead ghoul. Afraid of what he would find, Private First Class Chillcut reluctantly pulled the corpse off of the infant in the car seat, and then screamed *"Medic!"* at the top of his lungs. The orphaned baby kept screaming; miraculously she was unhurt.

*****

The sky over Fort Bragg faded from a brilliant blue to a burnt orange as the sun set. Little did Mike Desantos know that the next twenty-four hours would be the most difficult of his entire life. He ran the impending mission through his head as he watched four black helicopters of the 160th SOAR (Special Operations Aviation Regiment) bleed off airspeed, flare at the last moment and softly land in tight formation on the tarmac.

The show in the heavens was finishing its run with deep purples and blues slowly fading to black. Stars emerged, winking at those among the living willing to look up and imagine a world where the dead didn't roam.

Mike "Cowboy" Desantos walked with purpose to greet the Night Stalkers and bring the other eleven operators that would accompany him up to speed on this very important mission. He looked at the stars one last time and prayed to anyone listening to deliver his family to safety.

A few hours later, Mike and his Delta Operators were fully kitted out and ready to undertake Operation Eagle Aerie. The Delta Team call signs were Zulu One and Zulu Two. The MH-60G Pave

Hawks were given the call signs Reapers One and Two. Three and Four were the AH-64 Apache Longbows.

Walking towards the waiting flat black MH-60G Pave Hawk, Mike bowed under the spinning rotor and thought, *God help us all.*

Chapter 19
Day 2 -South Carolina

Carl turned right on State Route 17 that went east through downtown. At the intersection of Tadlock Road and State Route 17 they encountered a large group of the walking dead. The Denny's on the corner had more than ten of them milling around near the front doors. Terrified early morning diners were trapped inside the restaurant. Their faces were pressed against the glass as they witnessed the mayhem outside. In the parking lot there was a small car high centered on a mound of dead bodies. The front wheels were off of the ground and spun freely trying to get purchase. Carl slowed the Escalade and crept past. Some of the walkers took interest and tried to follow, while others had just succeeded in breaking a window on the compact car and were attacking the young couple through the opening. Harboring a feeling of helplessness, Carl glanced at his sister and registered the slight side to side shaking of her head. Stopping to help them was out of the question; discretion had to be the better part of valor if they wanted to survive. Brook held Raven's head in her lap as they passed by the gruesome scene.

They narrowly avoided colliding with a fast moving, out of control pickup thanks to Carl's quick reflexes. Instead it plowed into a string of parked cars in front of the Holiday Inn. Undead poured from the motel, swarming the ruined truck. After the near collision Carl recommended that Raven get buckled up in one of the back seats.

Three Myrtle Beach Police Department Ford Crown Victoria cruisers screeched to a stop between the Denny's and the motel. Without delay the zombies surrounded the police cars. In a scene that reminded Brook of the Rodney King riots in L.A., the three patrol cars roared away to safety, leaving the truck driver for dead. She supposed this would be the case in the next few days as society continued to disintegrate.

The news helicopter flitting around the downtown area reminded Carl to turn on the radio and scan for a transmitting station. WKNB AM was the only one on the air. They listened as they drove. The female reporter said President Bernard Odero was in a secure location but Vice President Chauncey Lindstrom was still in the District of Columbia; Speaker of the House Valerie Clay was in a separate and secure location. She went on to report that the Center for Disease Control in Atlanta was working around the clock to find a counter to the virus. So far they knew the mortality rate was one hundred percent. Any bite or saliva contact definitely led to infection; the pathogen was isolated to the mouth and bred and thrived there. The speed of its introduction into the blood stream depended on the location and severity of the bite on the victim's body. For instance, a bite on the neck near the jugular vein or carotid artery resulted in a quick death from loss of blood, consequently the time until reanimation was more rapid. Furthermore, she warned people to stay away from areas where large groups of people assembled, such as churches, hospitals and shopping malls. For quarantine reasons the main roads in and out of most cities would soon be closed as mandated by the CDC, Homeland Security and FEMA. Comfort centers had been established in some cities for the infected and their families.

Carl said aloud to no one in particular, "I wonder how long the upper levels of government have been in their comfort centers?" He sarcastically added, "I bet those fat cats have caviar and champagne where they are holed up."

Brook said, "Sounds to me like the flu or whatever it's called now is far more dangerous than anyone was reporting initially. I'd bet the government is already planning severe contingency plans if the spread isn't slowed or stopped soon."

"What measures do you think they'll resort to?" Carl wondered.

"I remember when Cade told me about a conspiracy theory web site he checked on occasion. He said there was talk about FEMA already having set aside hundreds of thousands of body bags in multiple locations around the continental United States."

"Where are they? Did Cade mention that?" Carl asked.

"No. It really disturbed me then. I remember he said that all of the locations were near rail lines..."

"That sure sounds like Nazi Germany and the Holocaust, not our United States government. Wow, really?" Carl intoned incredulously.

"Considering all of the things our government has swept under the rug or just plain lied about, I would put little past them," Brook said.

"I wholeheartedly agree, little sister."

Raven announced "I have to go pee," then asked her mom, "have you checked your phone to see if Dad called?"

"Not in a while. Where is that thing?" Her phone was at the bottom of her bag. She checked it. "No bars, Raven. It looks like there are no new messages either. We'll have to check again later."

They pulled over in a deserted Albertsons' parking lot so Raven could relieve her bladder. The dark store looked like it had recently been bombed. Trash and bodies littered the entryway and most of the ground level windows were reduced to glittering shards on the asphalt.

Raven exited the vehicle while Brook looked on, the shotgun cradled in the crook of her arm. It was the longest two minutes of Raven's young life as she squatted by the idling SUV.

One of the bodies near the storefront suddenly sat up and clumsily stood erect. Brook looked over at her daughter who was still peeing. "Hurry up. We have company."

The undead man creakily shuffled towards them. He was badly mauled, his intestines trailing behind him like a pet snake. Brook looked away in disgust. Raven buttoned up her jeans and jumped back into the Escalade in one motion.

For some reason Brook lingered outside of the vehicle.

"Get in Sis!" Carl yelled.

70

Brook shouldered her dad's shotgun and cocked one of the hammers. The thing was ten feet from the SUV when Carl blew the horn. Brook jumped and the gun discharged, blowing one frail looking arm off of the middle-aged walker. It kept a slow steady pace, still homing in on Brook.

The first mistake was Carl sounding the horn; the second was Brook missing the headshot. Fumbling to get the second hammer cocked, Brook looked past the intestine-dragging ghoul and counted a number of undead exiting the store.

Raven started screaming as the walkers converged on her mom. Their moaning quickly reached a terrifying crescendo.

Brook steadied her aim and silently cursed the undead being as she pulled the trigger. The shotgun blast pulped the walker's head; it fell and rolled, twisting itself up in its own entrails. The smells and sounds were overwhelming. Gagging, she hauled herself into the Escalade.

Carl floored it. Ignoring his own rule, he careened over a multitude of the walking dead on his way to the road. His mouth curled up at the corners as he silently scolded himself, *Note to self, no more honking the horn, Carl.*

Looking over at her brother, Brook noticed his inappropriate grin and asked him to share his thoughts. Carl declined at first. "You almost got me killed back there, Carl!" Brook halfheartedly screamed at him. Carl acquiesced. "I was just mentally scolding myself for honking the horn back there. It won't happen again."

"I owe you an apology. It wasn't the time or the place to test my courage," Brook said with a sheepish grin.

"Sis, if I'd known this is what it would take for us to get along so well, I would've wished for the zombie apocalypse a long time ago... minus what happened to Mom and Dad of course." Carl immediately wished he could take back his words.

While dodging more walkers, he maneuvered the truck in the direction of Interstate 17 and eventually Fort Bragg.

Chapter 20
Day 2 - Columbia River Gorge, Oregon

The encounter with the sheriff couldn't have ended better. Rawley followed Cade and the kids off of the highway at the next exit. Old River Road was the name of the route that wound along the east side of the Sandy River. It merged with and then turned into the Historic Columbia River Highway which was completed in 1922, allowing access to the scenic Columbia River Gorge. Many accessible waterfalls and hiking trails were scattered along the next 35 miles. It was beautiful country, lush and green with the shallow Sandy River meandering through the middle of it. It was an enticingly cool body of water that beckoned on a hot day like today.

Distancing themselves from a million potentially infected Portlanders seemed like a better idea than stopping to cool off. There wasn't a second to waste; travel would be slow on the twisty two-lane blacktop.

Ike's voice sounded from the backseat of the Sequoia. "Mom and ....." He started to say something and then he broke down and bawled. Once he was finally able to compose himself he finished what he was going to say. "Mom and Dad used to bring us here. I really miss them." Leo pulled his little brother close and silently comforted him.

After a few minutes of driving they passed a sign that read "Crown Point State Park next left." Cade steered the truck to the left and parked diagonally across the lines so he wouldn't get boxed in from behind. Rawley followed his lead and edged the Bronco next to the Sequoia.

A bright red convertible Volkswagen Cabriolet and a beautifully restored, canary yellow Camaro were parked in the Vista House parking lot.

"Stay in the truck and keep the doors locked. Rawley and I will take a look around. Honk if there are any problems," Cade instructed the boys.

The Vista House was a massive stone building in the shape of an octagon. It had floor to ceiling glass windows that afforded the best views up and down the wide Columbia River.

A pair of attractive young ladies stood by the stone retaining wall. They were looking to the west down the gorge, their long blond hair whipping about their heads. The gorge was famous for its beauty as well as its strong east wind. They were looking in the direction of Portland and taking turns using the type of coin-operated binoculars that are a fixture at tourist traps with a view. One of the girls caught Cade looking her way and asked him if he had any change. He thrust his hands in his pockets and pulled them both inside out. "No I don't, sorry," he replied.

"That's OK, we've probably seen enough... It's just that it looks like Portland is on fire," the girl using the binoculars said, her face still glued to the contraption.

Her visually stunning duplicate left to find some quarters; she tried to open the double glass doors of the Vista House only to find them locked. "That's strange, this place is still closed. The sign reads open 9 a.m. to 7 p.m. all days," the blonde said.

A sixtyish-looking man wearing a powder blue fisherman's hat emerged from around the building. He wore walking shorts and a long sleeved cotton shirt; his eyes were hidden behind a pair of big bulky "old people" sunglasses.

Cade asked the young women, who appeared to be twins, where they were from.

Almost in unison, the blondes answered.

"I'm Shelly."

"I'm her sister Sheila; we live in Portland."

Cade shook their hands one at a time. "My name's Cade. I used to live in Portland."

Rawley nodded to both women. "My name's Rawley, pleased to meet you. Which way are you lovely ladies headed?"

Shelly answered, "Sheila and I came from Hood River this morning. We stayed at the Gorge Hotel last night, got up and had breakfast in the restaurant. The waitress told us about some kind of mass murder that happened last night at one of the big apple orchards in the valley."

Then her twin Sheila interjected. "It freaked me out so much that I called our mom. I tried her and a few friends but I couldn't get ahold of anyone. I thought maybe it was just my crappy cell phone, so when the waitress came back I asked to use the hotel phone. She said the phones had been down since last night."

The other twin finished the story. "Now we're both kind of sketched out, the server drops our check and adds that she heard some of the murdered people had been partially eaten."

At the tail end of the story the older man in the fishing hat walked up and introduced himself as Harry Conrad, and shook hands with everyone.

"I couldn't help but overhear about people being eaten?" Harry said.

"I think the waitress was just embellishing. Good stories usually equal good tips... right?" Shelly said hopefully.

"Not in my book. I just wanted to add what I saw on the boob tube this morning. Some youths got out of hand yesterday and attacked cops and soldiers and innocent bystanders downtown. It was the craziest thing I have seen since those Kent State shootings. It looked like the National Guard was firing on the crowd."

"In Portland?" one of the blondes said, her voice laced with skepticism.

"Right there in the Courthouse Square... hell of a sight to watch. The news anchor also alluded to troubles, bite wounds and such, cropping up in some of the emergency rooms in and around Portland..."

The freight train roar of Harley Davidson motorcycles reverberating up the basalt canyon walls from the interstate two hundred yards below the Vista House cut Harry off before he could finish.

Looking over the edge, Cade and Rawley watched the horde of Harley Davidsons and SUVs speed east up the gorge. Cade lost count after 30 and then returned his attention to the conversation.

Rawley nudged Cade and said cryptically while looking at him over the top of his sunglasses, "Looks like the Sheriff opened the road."

"We better keep our eyes open for those bikers. Chances are that the Sheriff wasn't left with much of a choice," Cade said in a hushed voice.

"One man against that group... no way he could deny them passage. Not without a SWAT team," Rawley agreed.

The thought caused an icy ball to form in the pit of the former Delta Operator's stomach. He made a mental note to himself: *I need to get these kids somewhere and teach them how to handle the guns. We could use more shooters, especially if we get in a skirmish with a group of that size.*

Pointing west Harry asked, "Does anyone know what's causing all that smoke?"

Rawley answered with a serious look on his face. "Sir, I'd tell you, but I doubt that you'd believe me."

"What do you mean...?" Shelly asked.

"When you all leave here, turn on your radios. I promise this isn't any Orson Welles 'War of the Worlds' hoax. There is some credence to what Harry here just said about the city going to hell in a handbasket... and then some."

"We've got some road to burn up. Good luck to you all. If I were you I'd steer well clear of Portland," Cade said as he opened the door, held the grab handle near his head and climbed into the driver's seat.

"Is there a forest fire coming?" Leo queried worriedly.

"No, that's Portland. Surely the creatures are following the living that are fleeing the city and I can almost guarantee they will come this way," Cade answered Leo as he fired up the Toyota, adding, "Let's put some more miles between us and them." He stared at Leo and then at Ike before saying, "We need to find a place to teach you guys to shoot a pistol and maybe the shotgun."

They hit the road, Cade, Leo and Ike in the Sequoia and Rawley driving solo in his Bronco. Harry and the two women were still having an animated conversation in the parking lot. Rawley watched them in his rear view mirror until they were but tiny specks.

The two vehicle convoy exited the Vista House parking lot, veered left and continued east on the scenic highway. Leo passed out energy bars and bottled water as they wound through the back roads of the Columbia River Gorge.

Cade commented, "Later on we'll stop so we can eat some real food," then he caught himself. "I guess calling an MRE real food is stretching it a bit. I'll let you judge for yourselves," he said with a chuckle.

Back at the Vista House, just minutes after Cade, Rawley and the boys made their exit, a man in a Dodge Ram pickup arrived and pulled up next to the Camaro and VW. The man looked the three over before rolling down his window and greeting them.

"How are y'all doing? My name is Duncan, Duncan Winters." He had a nasally Southern twang which matched his ruddy complexion. His Stetson hat and squinting wise eyes made him seem one hundred percent cowboy.

Harry removed his dark glasses and extended his hand upwards towards Duncan and made his acquaintance.

The twins introduced themselves.

"Sheila Olsen, hi," she said, smoothing her hair behind her ear.

"I'm Shelly Olsen." She greeted him with a wave of her small hand.

Duncan stayed in his truck with the window rolled down, letting the engine idle and proceeded to recount what he had just witnessed thirty minutes ago.

The twins were visibly shaken. Harry shook his head slowly side to side, staring at the ground.

Shelly broke the silence. "I think we saw them heading east a couple of minutes ago," remembering the pack of noisy motorcycles.

"Looks like I'm not going back to Portland any time soon" Harry remarked glumly.

Sheila opined, "I think we ought to go the same way those two trucks just went. What do you think Sis?"

Before Shelly could add her opinion, Duncan Winters told them he was going to head east and see if he could find a lawman to make things right for the murdered little girl. "If the law isn't around these parts any longer, then I may have to take things into my own hands."

When the cowboy finished Shelly finally answered her sister with a silent nod of agreement.

They all headed eastbound on the Columbia River Gorge scenic highway. Harry's yellow Camaro took the lead with the little red convertible in the middle and the dually 4x4 pickup driven by Duncan bringing up the rear. Duncan couldn't help but obsess about the poor little girl and how horribly she had suffered. He was sure there was a special place in hell for monsters like the ones that butchered her. Duncan had indirectly sent his fair share of them there himself during the Vietnam War, and he had not a shred of remorse. *If only I get a chance,* he thought as he kept an eye on the road behind him.

Chapter 21
Day 2 - Wahkeena Falls, Columbia River Gorge, Oregon

The two truck procession wheeled into the Wahkeena Falls parking lot. There were roughly twenty parking spots and a one way circular drive all ringed by tall fir trees. In the middle of the drive was an expanse of green grass with a number of picnic tables arranged near the center. A small white school bus with a bright yellow "Little Learners Preschool" logo on the door occupied the spot nearest the trailhead.

The bathrooms were built to resemble miniature log cabins. Beyond the bathrooms a trail snaked down gradually about a quarter of a mile to the waterfall. The summer before last, when he was home from deployment, Cade and Raven had a father and daughter outing here. He remembered the falls were beautiful, but rather small and unimpressive. It seemed a perfectly safe and short hike to take a group of preschoolers on.

Except for the bus, the lot was empty.

Cade backed the Sequoia into a parking spot near the preschool bus. Rawley slid the Bronco in right next to it. They all got out and stretched their legs. Ike ran and played on the grass in the middle of the parking lot, and Leo chased him around the picnic tables; finally his longer legs prevailed and he scooped up his wiry brother and tickled him until he cried uncle. The two boys continued to playfully wrestle each other.

Cade looked on, awed by the boys' resilience. Their mom and dad had just died and the trauma had drawn them closer to each other. To survive they would have to have each other's backs at all times. The scene choked him up and made him long to hold his family again. He composed himself and called the boys over.

"Times a' wasting, let's eat."

Cade wanted to eat quickly and continue on. The need to reunite with his family was stronger than ever.

They all assembled at the open rear of the Sequoia. Ike passed out the MREs (meals ready to eat) from the case calling out the flavors as he grabbed them.

"Leo gets chicken à la King."

"Mmmm," Leo said, inspecting the olive drab bag.

"Cade gets spaghetti and meatballs." Ike tossed him the package.

"What. I don't get to choose?"

"Take it or leave it," Ike said matter-of-factly, grinning at Cade.

"Rawley, what do you want? Chili-mac... or sweet and sour pork?" he asked next, showing off both identical looking packaged meals.

"I'll take the swine, thanks Ike." Rawley snatched the one he suspected might be his.

"You give *him* a choice now?" Cade said, feigning a hurt look.

"Just playin' with you." Ike opened the leftover chili-mac. It was the one he secretly wanted anyway.

The boys were amazed by the self-heating MREs; you just added a tablespoon of water and waited for a couple of minutes, grabbed a spoon and dug in.

"Not bad at all," Ike stated through a mouthful.

After everyone had finished with their meals it was time for gun training. Normally Cade wouldn't advocate discharging a firearm in a state park, but normal went out the window when the dead started to walk.

One at a time, Cade checked the magazines for the Glocks. Satisfied that they both held seventeen rounds, he inserted the mags and chambered a round in each pistol. Next he put on the combat harness and nestled each Glock in its holster. He hefted the matte black Mossberg 590 Roadblocker; it was a mean-looking 12 gauge shotgun. He loaded eight shells into the weapon alternating between shot and slug.

With the gun on safe, he called Ike and Leo over. Holding it up so they could see, he pointed out the safety, where the spent shells were ejected and how you loaded the ammunition. He also stressed, "You *never* point a gun at someone unless you are willing to use it on them." Keeping his finger to the side of the trigger guard he demonstrated how to carry the gun properly, barrel pointing towards the ground. Cade handed the gun to Leo with the safety on, being careful to practice what he preached.

"Point it towards the tree and show us what you've got!"

With some apparent trepidation Leo put the gun to his shoulder. Rawley called out, "Hold it firm against your shoulder and gently squeeze the trigger. Remember they do tend to kick."

The shotgun boomed. The recoil knocked the 5-foot-5 teen on his butt. Shredded leaves fluttered down from the tall oak tree.

"Alriiggghhhttt!!" yelled Leo.

"Kicks a little more than your PlayStation," Rawley said, bugging his eyes out and mugging at the boys.

"Yeah, hurt my shoulder too," Leo said as he rubbed the tender spot.

*****

Standing in the eddy of the falls, the group of undead had been mesmerized by the small fish swimming there. They clumsily stumbled and splashed around in the water pursuing the fingerling trout. A few of the little undead preschoolers had actually caught some of the fish, consuming them hungrily.

Barely audible over the noise of the rushing water, the gunfire caught the attention of the twelve undead preschoolers and their two undead chaperones. In unison they all started moving toward the sound of the shooting. Somehow instinctually they knew there was a connection between the noises in the distance and the possibility of food.

Following the little ghouls, the obese woman trudged up the trail towards the commotion. The wet sweat pants the undead woman wore sloshed with each plodding step. Literally on Norma's heels, the legless Stu pulled himself out of the water, through gravel and mud and slowly trailed after. His shattered femurs carved wet bloody furrows in the dusty path.

*****

The day before, during their short hike to the bottom of Wahkeena Falls, Norma had been moving a little slower than usual, and Lord knows Stu regularly got after her to pick up the pace.

In addition to her preschool job, Norma worked on the night shift at Providence Hospital in Portland. At the end of her shift the previous evening, a severely dehydrated patient had bitten her on the finger. She had been swabbing water in the man's mouth and he lunged forward with a wild look in his eyes and nicked her finger. The bite barely broke the skin. They cleaned the wound and gave her a tetanus shot. Norma had been feeling sick ever since.

*****

Norma was sitting on the bench by the water's edge when she passed out and stopped breathing. Stu struggled but couldn't find a pulse through her fat. He tried, but he couldn't summon the strength to move her three hundred pound body from the bench.

Not sure of what to do, Stu rounded up the kids and was preparing to go get help. While his back was turned Norma slowly stood up, her eyes glassy and staring; she started a low guttural moaning. Stu was so startled he nearly had a heart attack. When he touched her skin just a minute ago it was cold and lifeless, now she was standing before his eyes. Stu blinked not once, but multiple times. He went so far as to shake his head vigorously, but none of these actions changed reality. He tried to protect the kids from Norma and herd them up the path to safety. In the process he slipped on a moss covered rock and sprained his knee.

Norma went after the nearest kid, focusing on a four-year-old named Becky. The tots couldn't comprehend what had happened to their teacher. They didn't know what to do, but instinctively followed Stu's earlier instructions and stayed close to him. They became easy prey.

Teacher Norma killed Becky first, and fed on her little corpse until it reanimated. By now the kids were really confused and terrified at the same time. They huddled together beneath one of the many towering Douglas fir trees.

The undead woman and the recently reanimated Becky ruthlessly attacked the cowering four- and five-year-olds. In no time they were all dying or dead. Norma and Becky resumed chasing fish while the rest eventually turned.

During the murderous assault, Stu concealed himself as deep as he could in the green ferns beside the trail. He was unable to fit his whole body beneath the foliage but he waited, still and silent, hoping the zombie troop would leave the area. A dull throbbing in his knee was his undoing. Stu tried to straighten his leg ever so slowly to afford his tweaked knee some relief. *I hope Norma leads those little monsters somewhere soon,* he thought as he worked the kinks out of his muscles. Stu wondered why the creatures out there had seemingly forgotten all about him.

It started in the toes of his injured leg, a slight tingling that radiated up his Achilles tendon to his hamstring; it felt like the muscle was being twisted by a four hundred pound gorilla. White hot pain shot to his brain as his leg seized up on its own. It was the mother of all charley horses and Stu instinctively forced his leg to straighten. A rock the size of a golf ball squirted from under the waffled sole of his boot and rolled across the trail in the direction of the monsters, a handful of pebbles followed and skittered onto the path piquing their attention. Soon he was set upon by the undead kids; they started to eat him feet first. The little creatures looked like piglets lined up on the momma sow's teats as they worked their heads back and forth removing the flesh from Stu's legs. No one heard his screams echoing through the gorge as he bled to death in the underbrush. Stu reanimated minutes later.

*****

Ike declined to shoot the Mossberg after the ass kicking it gave his brother. Cade went over the important aspects of safe shooting with the boy. Ike was in the process of aiming the Glock pistol at the water bottles Rawley had lined up, when in his peripheral vision he saw the first of the little walkers emerge from the trees near the bathrooms. It was a barefoot, towheaded boy, clothed in a blood drenched Thomas the Train shirt and muddy blue jeans.

Ike instantly forgot everything he had just been told, the gun in his hand automatically following his turning head.

Cade and Rawley backpedaled to get away from the moving muzzle.

By the time everyone was aware of the little zombies, they had all emerged from around both sides of the white bus. When they saw Ike and the others they started to moan and shamble directly for them.

As fast as his finger could pull the trigger, Ike emptied the seventeen bullets from the magazine. The reports echoed loudly, but unfortunately not one bullet found a target.

Leo and Ike each leapt on top of the nearest picnic table. Ike stared at the useless Glock with its slide locked open. The first of the ambling kids reached the table that Leo was on top of, moaning and hissing, its arms flailing, struggling to grab ahold of him. The little ghouls were much faster than the other walkers the group had encountered so far.

Rawley had a clear path to his truck; he sprinted to the passenger side door, jerked it open and lunged across the bench seat for his rifle. Cold little hands clutched onto his leg. Turning onto his back, he saw someone's little undead angel about to bite him. Fortunately he was able to wedge the tip of his boot into her open mouth. He pressed the SKS barrel to the top of her head and watched the thing gnaw on his boot. Careful to aim up and away from his toes, he pulled the trigger once. The little forehead absorbed the bullet and the rear of its skull blew off, depositing chunks of brain on the ground. He used the smoking barrel of the SKS to pry the ghoul's jaws open and extricate her teeth from his boot. A noticeable wet bite mark was left behind. *Thank God for steel toed boots.*

Cade methodically fired his M4 across the hood of his truck; precise headshots dropped two of the undead tots next to their preschool bus; three more fell at the trailhead.

Ike and Leo had each attracted two of the undead kids and were anxiously playing keep away from them atop the picnic tables.

Rawley painted the red laser beam on the two nearest to Ike. Careful to avoid friendly fire he shot one round at each of their little skulls. One after the other they dropped to the grass. Blood leaked from the fatal head wounds and pooled around their bodies.

Ike leapt over another little walker; she turned a clumsy pirouette while groping at thin air. A short sprint and Ike was in the Sequoia unscathed.

Doing his best Walter Peyton impersonation, Leo hurdled over the zombies converging on him. He joined his brother in the Sequoia and slammed the door behind him.

"Where the eff did those things come from?"

"I don't know, Ike, but even though Mom and Dad aren't here you still have to watch your mouth."

"I said eff, not the actual word."

"You know what I mean little bro. I can't believe we are arguing about some cursing when there are dead little kids walking around outside." Leo continued on, making it clear he was the boss now. "Just don't forget what they would expect from us now. If you do I *will* help you remember."

Cade was in the process of reloading his M4 when the rest of the walkers made him their target.

Rawley started his Bronco, engaged the transmission, tromped the accelerator and aimed the truck at the group headed in Cade's direction. Three of them disappeared underneath the front bumper, tiny limbs twisted askew before being brutally ejected out the back. Rawley wheeled around and drove over the top of the little corpses once more for good measure.

Cade finished reloading and started walking toward the vehicles. The tiny bodies strewn about the parking lot made for a grotesque obstacle course to negotiate.

"Thanks Rawley, those little ones sure do scoot, don't they?" Cade said as he stepped over a mangled four-year-old. "We're even now right?"

"You bet, buddy. I would be still holed up in my house… or something's dinner if it weren't for your help this morning. I am forever grateful."

Chapter 22
Day 2 - Carolina Shores, South Carolina

Carl threaded the Escalade through the remaining undead roaming the Albertsons parking lot and then turned northeast on US Route 17.

Fort Bragg, North Carolina was roughly 150 miles away if they went via the large main thoroughfares. He decided to circumvent the populated ocean front by staying on back roads and then cross into North Carolina on one of the rural routes that were less likely to be blocked by the Carolina National Guard.

Raven was sitting up and taking in the scenery along Frontage Road. There were still pockets of undead but their numbers diminished the farther they traveled away from Myrtle Beach.

Carl swerved the SUV around the larger groups of undead but couldn't resist giving the lone walkers "love taps" with the Escalade. Every thump of Cadillac and zombie colliding provided Carl a little satisfaction. After seeing the little car high centered with the occupants surrounded by the undead horde, Carl did his best to avoid running over any zombies lest they befall the same fate. Even though the Cadillac was much bigger and had more ground clearance, if enough of them went underneath and got stuck he would be forced to stop and clear them out. There was also the outside chance of a big femur or tibia bone puncturing one of the tires and forcing them to stop and try to put on the spare, potentially leaving them surrounded.

In his peripheral vision Carl noticed the sun flash off of the speeding car a second before impact. The interior of the Cadillac erupted with a whirlwind of flying glass and the horrible sound of compacting sheet metal. Before they could even comprehend what had just happened, the airbags exploded, leaving all of the windows obscured. The big luxury SUV spun three full revolutions before coming to a stop in the middle of the far right lane and then it rocked back and forth on its suspension for a short duration.

Carl came to. His head throbbed , his back was killing him and he had momentarily forgotten where he was. The silence was eerie. White powder from the deployed airbags swirled around his face reminding him of feathers floating in the air after a pillow fight.

Brook had taken a blow to the head when it bounced off of the passenger side glass. She was fortunate to have suffered only a mild concussion. Most of the windows were now in thousands of tiny pieces all over the road and the inside of the SUV.

Brook's first instinct was to look for Raven. Her little girl was curled into a ball on the floor of the third row of seats. Raven coughed and called out for her mom.

In the seconds after impact Carl shook his head and felt his extremities checking for anything broken. Satisfied there weren't any nonworking parts, he looked out through the imploded windows for any threats. A midsized, black 6 Series BMW sat fifty feet away leaking fluids, smoke starting to billow from the engine compartment.

As the airbag powder finished settling in the SUV's interior, Carl asked his sister and niece if they were OK. Waving the dust from in front of her face, Brook replied, "I've had better days. My head *really* hurts." From the back of the Escalade Raven continued calling for her mom. Brook unbuckled her belt and crawled into the backseat to reassure her daughter and check her over for injuries.

Still surveying the intersection, Carl noticed a handful of the undead on the other side of the now burning BMW. He turned his attention to the occupants of the car; the passenger had just started stirring. The driver was slumped over the deflated airbag.

"Brook, get Raven out and cover me with the shotgun. I'm going to check on those people," Carl said, pointing towards the wreck.

He found that running wasn't easy. The violent impact had caused his knees to knock together and they both hurt like hell.

Arriving at the Beemer's passenger side Carl tried to open the door. It was jammed shut by the crumpled metal around the frame. The dazed passenger pleaded, "Save my wife, please!"

Carl circled the car, taking note of about a dozen walkers half a block away. One look at the woman in the driver's seat said it all. Her head was misshapen and her skull was visible where her scalp had been peeled back; blood trickled from her ears and nose. He was about to make another effort to extricate the man when a whooshing sound and a blast of superheated air came from under the car, followed by angry flames licking up the doors.

Carl hobbled backwards, hands up warding off the intense heat and then rejoined his sister and niece. He watched the man in the BMW cross himself as the undead walkers arrived at the car. Oblivious to the searing heat they attacked the passenger's head and upper body, rending chunks of flesh off of him with their teeth and hands. Fully aware of his fate, the man emitted a high pitched warbling howl that turned into shrieks as they continued ripping into him.

Taking advantage of the BMW occupant's unwitting sacrifice, the three left the ruined SUV and made for the sprawling industrial buildings on the other side of the highway. Behind them a loud secondary explosion rocked the intersection, scattering and setting a number of the zombies afire. Still, a few of the walkers took chase.

Dodging the light traffic, they safely made their way across all six lanes. Carl held Raven's hand as Brook lugged the shotgun and her shoulder bag. Some of the dead weren't as lucky crossing the roadway. Looking back, Brook was relieved to see half of the pursuers get mowed down by a speeding passenger car.

A sign on the first building they happened upon read "Gunderson Tile Works." The door was locked and the metal garage door was closed. On they went deeper into the business park, the undead still hunting them, their moaning and stench carried on the wind.

Brook rounded the corner and caught a whiff of rotten flesh. There was an undead man in coveralls sitting on its butt; it was holding a human leg and gnawing on the foot. Lying near the feeding ghoul was a one-legged corpse dressed in the same type of coveralls; the logo read "Grimes Heating and Cooling."

The open garage door beckoned to the fleeing trio. The sign above also read "Grimes Heating and Cooling," and in small print right below it read "Specializing in Rooftop Installation."

Noise discipline went out the window; Brook shot the zombie in the face at pointblank range before it could stand up. Everything evaporated from the neck up. The now decapitated corpse rolled over and lay unmoving next to its deceased co-worker.

Brook followed Carl and Raven into the building. Carl grabbed the chain next to the door and pulled it hand over hand until the door kissed the ground with a metallic clang.

"Raven, come this way and stay behind me," Brook said while she felt for the light switch. The smell of death wasn't as bad inside the building. Interior details emerged as their eyes adjusted to the dimly lit garage. Most of the bay was occupied by a very large, bright red, industrial truck with a forty foot cherry picker basket on top. The "Grimes Heating and Cooling" logo was painted on the truck's door. Boxes were stacked everywhere. Some of the boxes were open revealing tin pipes used for HVAC installations.

Carl felt for the door knob and intuitively groped up and to the left for the light switch. With an audible click, then a hiss followed by a faint hum, the overhead fluorescents warmed up.

More was revealed. Heavily frosted skylights were spaced in intervals on the ceiling. A glass window with closed metal mini blinds was next to the closed office door. Around the back of the small office were two vending machines, one full of snacks and candy and the other containing cold beverages. A closed door presumably led deeper into the building.

Brook opened the breech of the Ithaca and replaced the spent round with a new 12 gauge shot shell. She then opened the door and cautiously ventured into what turned out to be a large storeroom, gun barrel leading the way. Satisfied the building was walker free, Brook sat down heavily on a plastic folding chair. Raven plopped on the floor by her feet, sighing loudly and laying her cheek on her mom's thigh.

Brook asked Carl, "How long do you think we're going to be safe in here?" As if in response to her question a series of loud bangs made her visibly jump. Her nerves shot, she flipped the source of the banging the finger. Raven whimpered.

"I figure the garage door will hold for a while, it's the small side door that worries me." Carl started sliding a box containing a large commercial air conditioning unit towards the small door. Brook and Raven added some muscle and together they positioned it in front of the door, and then for good measure they piled still more boxes on top of the larger one.

Carl ran his hands over the door. "This is a steel core door; it's the frame and hinges we have to worry about. It'll only take a few of those things to forget about the roll up door and start in on this one. If they do we are hosed."

Carl checked the door to the internal office. Finding it locked, he kicked the door. The wood around the lock splintered and the door flew inward. He flicked on the light and looked around the twenty by twenty foot room.

BANG.

A cheap particle board desk sat in the center of the room. They rifled through the drawers and found a number of full key rings.

BANG. BANG.

The zombies wanted in bad.

BANG. BANG.

"While I try these keys in the truck can you two unload the vending machines?" Carl tossed the keys labeled as "Soda/Candy." They fell near Brook's feet and she scooped them up.

Carl tried the keys in the truck's ignition while Brook and Raven looted both vending machines.

BANG.

The garage door moved inward, partially buckling under the pressing weight of the dead. Apparently Carl's theory about the strength of the garage door was being severely tested.

Having tried half of the keys, Carl finally found the right one. He turned the ignition slightly, and the noisy seatbelt warning bell chimed intermittently. He quickly turned the key to off. Talking over the persistent pounding, Carl explained how they were going to extricate themselves from the fix they were currently in.

Brook would drive the five ton truck with Carl in the bucket. This was necessary because someone tall and possessing good upper body strength would have to pull the chain to work the garage door up. The process would take him about thirty seconds, he estimated, based on the time it took to close the door when they arrived. Pulling the chain while standing on the ground would be suicide; the undead would flood the garage as soon as the crack under the door was big enough. Brook and Raven would occupy the cab of the truck and lay flat on the bench seat to avoid notice until the door was open far enough to allow their egress. If all went well they would pull out of the garage with Carl riding in the bucket and then drive to a safe place and let him in the cab.

Chapter 23
Day 2 - Wahkeena Falls, Columbia River Gorge, Oregon

Cade, Rawley, Leo and Ike were about to get back on the road when the obese undead woman made her appearance. The soaked clothing she wore left a wet trail behind her as she slowly plodded towards them. Cade shouldered his M4 rifle and aimed at the ghoul's forehead. He still couldn't distance himself enough from the fact that these things had once been someone's mom, dad, sister, kids... especially the kids.

Shooting the zombie kids was ten times harder than killing his undead neighbors Ted and Lisa. What amazed Cade was that he actually felt empathy for who the undead used to be. He found the longer he was removed from active duty and running ops, the more emotions began to manifest in him when he was forced to defend himself.

*****

When Cade arrived in country during his first tour in Iraq, he had an internal giddy anticipation of what combat was going to be like. He would have been lying if he said he wasn't just a little curious about what it would feel like to kill another man. His questions were answered within a week of being on the ground.

*****

The patrol Cade was on was supposed to be a routine daylight show of force. Six up-armored Humvees and the squad of Rangers were ordered to patrol a series of canals in the El-Anbar province. Mortars had been lobbed from the area the night before. They were going to bang on some doors and search some hovels looking for weapons or caches of explosives. They were on an elevated canal road when the Humvee in front of them disappeared in a cloud of fine dust and black smoke. The convoy halted. Their escape from the kill zone was limited because of the water-filled irrigation ditches on each side of the road. RPGs sailed over the Humvee with their telltale whooshing sound. The distinctive rattle of AK-47's and PKR belt fed machine guns entered the fray. All hell was breaking loose. The radio operator was calmly calling for Apache gunships and any available aviation assets to provide close air support.

A cacophony of fire from the turret mounted Ma-Deuce, M2 .50 caliber machine guns added to the decibel level. Cade was scanning his sector from his rear passenger window. A group of three insurgents in their traditional man dresses were crouched down and fumbling with what appeared to be a twelve volt car battery. The wires snaked atop the ground near the men and then dove under the sand, emerging near the dirt berm two meters from his Humvee. Without hesitation Cade sighted on the insurgents through the ACOG scope attached to his M4 carbine. In the split second it took him to acquire them with the scope he ascertained that the men were trying to attach wires to the battery; Cade guessed they had failed to detonate one of the roadside IEDs on their first attempt.

For Cade, everything slowed down and his senses were heightened. He felt a super awareness wash over him. He could see the three very clearly through the magnified scope and they were fully aware they were going to meet their maker. A surprised look registered on the nearest insurgent's face as the bullets tore into him and caused him to crumple over the battery, wires still in hand. The other two terrorists ignored their comrade's act of martyrdom, rolled his body away and continued on with the task. Cade admired their tenacity, realizing that they were trying to finish the job they had started. He sighted on the man holding the wires and shot him three times in center mass. The fatal 5.56 hardball broke apart upon impact and tumbled through his body shredding muscle, lung and intestine before lodging in his liver. The remaining man tried to detonate the bomb. He was furiously clicking something with both hands when the Ranger to Cade's right killed him with a sustained burst from his M-249 SAW. The tango's body folded over backwards at an unusual angle.

The *whump, whump, whump* sound of the Apache gunship's rotor blades filled the air. Another insurgent materialized from the canal. He was looking up, searching for the source of the hated sound when a three round burst from Cade's rifle struck him in the throat and chin, effectively ending his ability to wage jihad. The Apache gunship orbited overhead, the continuous fire from its nose-mounted cannon decimating the rest of the attackers.

In the end, two of their Humvee gun trucks were destroyed and they suffered four KIA, all from the lead vehicle. Six more soldiers were wounded gravely enough to warrant being medivacked.

In the aftermath of the ambush the Explosive Ordinance Disposal experts confirmed that the wires were indeed affixed to two 120mm mortar shells intended to destroy the other vehicles stranded on the berm by the first destroyed Humvee. Cade's quick thinking and precise fire saved the rest of his squad from certain destruction and earned him a Bronze Star in the process. He also learned that day, to his relief, that he derived no pleasure from killing another human being. He did, however, feel no remorse over taking an enemy combatant's life.

*****

Wahkeena Falls

Cade put the scope to his eye; the female walker's pasty white form filled the reticle. A single shot to the forehead dropped her body to the gravel path.

*****

Eat, feed, want..., eat, feed, want..., eat, feed, want.... It was the mantra of the living dead, the cadence drumming autonomously from the instinct-driven part of his brain. He possessed no memories, feelings, or true desires. That part of his brain died when he did. The only urge left in him was to eat, feed, want... and it propelled the legless husk that used to be Stu up the shallow incline from the scene of his first death. Clawing...eat, pulling...feed, inching...wanting to get to the sounds that meant food.

*****

Cade had the unenviable task of searching the dead creature's clothes for the keys to the van. They were in the front pocket of her wet sweat pants, much too close to her crotch for his liking. After extracting the keys he tossed them to Ike and told him to check the locked van for anything they could use. Surely there would be food and drink they could liberate.

Ike obliged, and while the kid searched the bus Cade reloaded the shotgun and the magazines for the other weapons. Rawley followed suit.

Ike tossed the sack lunches onto the ground and went back for the cooler which contained little milk cartons that were still cool. The Coleman cooler was awkward to lug out of the bus, but he struggled with it in the stifling heat until it was on the pavement of the parking lot. Catching his breath on the bottom step in the stairwell of the bus, Ike let his legs dangle as he ate a peanut butter and jelly sandwich and drank a carton of cool milk. He called out to the others, held up his drink and asked if they wanted some. Mid-sentence he let out a yelp that escalated into a piercing scream.

Stu's teeth tore into Ike's Achilles tendon; blood soaked his sock and coursed into his sneaker. Ike fell from the stair onto the hot pavement face first and the legless creature crawled on top of him.

Leo, Cade and Rawley sprinted across the grassy median to his aid. Leo arrived first and proceeded to kick at the legless corpse, screaming hoarsely in fear and rage. Rawley yelled for the others to stand back, and then put two rounds from his SKS into the side of the ghoul's head.

Grimacing from the pain, Ike freed his legs from under the motionless thing that had just bitten him. He shed his Converse first and then removed the blood drenched tube sock. Ike started to cry when the extent of the damage was revealed. The grim recognition crossed Rawley's mind that Ike was as good as dead.

Chapter 24
Day 2 - Carolina Shores, South Carolina

Brook turned the ignition and the motor throbbed to life. It was by far the biggest vehicle she had ever driven. Outside the banging intensified as the ghouls responded to the engine noise. They had been hammering nonstop since the three took refuge an hour ago. There were so many hungry walkers outside that their combined weight had begun to compress the door inward.

Carl was inside the bucket and held the chain. Hand over hand he began pulling it towards him. With the added weight of the walkers on the door it was much harder to get moving. As soon as the door parted from the floor the undead began spilling into the enclosed area. The more he struggled to open the garage door, the harder the bucket bobbed up and down. The movement alerted the swarming corpses of his presence. The door rose slowly while the undead moaned and swiped at Carl bouncing just inches from their gnarled fingers. Before long there were two dozen walkers jammed into the small space; their stench coupled with the truck's exhaust was quickly becoming toxic. Some of the undead clambered up onto the sides of the bucket truck, leaving greasy slug tracks with their decaying bodies. As the last couple of feet of door gave way to sunlight, Carl banged on the roof of the rig with the shotgun's barrel. He hoped there was enough clearance to make their getaway; if not, he was going to be several inches shorter.

Brook popped up and mashed the throttle under her foot. With only an inch to spare, the commercial vehicle leapt out of the tall garage and into the roadway of the business park. It was an automatic and far easier to drive than Brook had anticipated. It was no sports car but she could still muscle the thing where she wanted it to go.

Two of the undead were still holding onto the truck when Carl popped up from the bucket, shotgun in hand. The ghouls focused their attention on Brook and Raven in the truck's cab and together started banging on the side windows, their pulpy decaying hands leaving a gray sheen that clouded the glass. Carl's first shot peppered one ghoul with buckshot, but still the undead teenage girl held fast. On the passenger side the older male, missing a few fingers on each hand, was slowly losing purchase on the speeding truck.

Brook tried to shake them off by swerving back and forth in the narrow street. The undead male lost his battle to hang on, bounced off of a small compact car and then impacted the cement. It tried to stand on two broken legs only to collapse back to the roadway. It crawled in the direction of the truck, the unyielding desire for flesh its only master.

The young undead girl by the driver's side window looked up at Carl. This made for a perfect target. The last shell in the shotgun was a slug; it tore through the ghoul's skull and destroyed the thing's brain. Dead again she hung limply, arm caught in the truck's side mirror.

Brook didn't so much as flinch after the last shot and was relieved to see the gaping hole in the thing's head. Each bump Brook hit in the road caused it to bob up and down, scattering chunks of brain along the way.

Raven cautiously peered over the top of the dash before sitting up. Her knuckles were white from clutching the door handle. "Where are we going now?" she asked timorously.

"We are heading towards the state line. The route south of here should be the safest, but first things first, we need to pull over and let your uncle in the cab."

The roads were still lightly traveled and it appeared people were staying put in their houses. When the president declared martial law and FEMA issued their directive it was still well before the major rush hour. However, the drivers that were on the road had to be avoided because they were failing to obey basic rules of the road.

Brook was still very sore from the violent collision with the BMW and she couldn't shake the vision of the burning couple pinned in the car as they died.

All of the stores they passed had been closed. A couple of gas stations were open, but the lined up cars were a bad sign. They traveled two miles with Carl bouncing up and down in the bucket before a safe place to pull over presented itself.

Gravel crunched under the bucket truck's tires as it slowed down on the shoulder of International Drive.

Carl gingerly climbed out of the bucket cradling the shotgun. He was green and on the verge of throwing up for the second time today. He jumped in the passenger seat. Not wanting to be chauvinistic, he insisted Brook keep on driving. He fished the ammunition from Brook's bag and reloaded the Ithaca.

"That was the scariest ride of my life," Raven said.

"Try it from my perspective; those things thought I was a meat piñata."

"I thought we were done for back there," Brook said, her eyes looking up to check the rear view mirror before adding, "We need more firepower."

The discussion morphed into how they should get to Fort Bragg. It was decided if they could get to the 90 with no problems then they would have to brave the interstate for a scant few miles before getting back on the less traveled roads.

Brook looked down at the gas gauge and was overwhelmed by a feeling of dread when she saw the needle pegged on empty. "Everybody keep a look out for a gas station or a store that might have some garden supplies."

Raven looked at her quizzically but didn't ask.

"I remember that there was a Bi-Mart around here somewhere," Carl said.

They neared the 90 and the traffic increased. Sure enough at the four-way intersection stood the Bi-Mart as well as a Target and a truck stop that doubled as a gas station/mini-mart combination. A man with some kind of an assault rifle was protecting the pumps. A pile of unmoving corpses were stacked up on the grass in the shadow of a large white propane tank.

On the other side of the street stood an unguarded Target store. People were streaming in and out with stolen goods, filling up all manner of vehicles. It was the most orderly looting they had ever seen.

Brook pulled the truck in behind the Bi-Mart. They were lucky that looters usually preferred to take the path of least resistance. Like almost any Bi-Mart in the United States this one had short hours. When they closed they buttoned their stores up, save for the potted plants, bark dust and bagged fertilizer left outside overnight. The entrances were protected with roll down metal security doors that even obscured the few windows on the storefront.

"I have an idea."

"Do tell," Carl said as he looked across Raven, in the middle of the bench seat, directly at Brook.

"Do you think you can figure out how to operate the bucket on this beast?"

"I'm sure it's pretty basic," Carl answered.

"Then we're going to break in from the roof, quickly take what we need and be on our way," Brook said, making her plan sound way too easy.

"What can I do?"

"Raven, you have the most important task. While your Mom and I are in the store you will be our eyes and ears. Walk the perimeter of the roof and be on the lookout for walking corpses or real live people. If there are any changes in their number or if they start acting funny, call down to us. Remember to keep a low profile while you are up there."

She looked worried. Carl knew the stresses of running and surviving were weighing heavily on all of them. He figured that by simply giving her a task it might keep her mind occupied, leaving less time to dwell on the day's events.

There were no undead in sight as Brook backed the cherry picker close to the exterior wall of the building.

Carl exited the vehicle, shotgun in hand. Back in the bucket again, he looked the controls over. One lever controlled up and down movement. Another was labeled telescope, extend and retract. The third was a lever to control the boom's rotation.

He yelled, "Get up here both of you!"

Brook locked the truck and pocketed the keys.

They were all crowded in the bucket. Carl manipulated the levers, bouncing them around like they were in a carnival ride. He suspected it was easier to fly a helicopter than get this arm to do what he wanted. After three attempts and a scrape or two on the wall the bucket was close enough for them to climb onto the roof. Once on top Raven started to patrol the four sides of the roof while Brook and Carl tried their hand at breaking and entering. Carl surveyed the expansive roof. A bulky air conditioning unit jutted up in the middle of two rows of skylights. The heavily frosted glass panes were embedded with chicken wire for protection against intruders much like them.

Giving Raven fair warning Carl said, "I have to break the glass. The noise might draw some unwanted attention. Keep your eyes peeled."

"OK," she called back, then gave them a security update. "The back lot is still empty."

Carl raised the weapon and bashed it butt first into the window. The shotgun stock was solid walnut and much stronger than the glass. With a loud crack the pane shattered but stayed in the frame. A couple of well-placed kicks sent the whole thing tumbling down into the dimly lit store.

Carl contemplated the distance to the floor; he called Brook over to solicit her opinion. They agreed that it would be roughly a twelve foot drop if Carl was hanging by his hands from the open skylight. If there were any undead in the store the crashing glass should have brought them around to investigate. He waited for five minutes and then decided to go for it.

Raven walked the perimeter of the roof while still keeping a low profile. The desperate people at Target were still cleaning it out; the calm was broken by sporadic gunfire. The people looting the store were now getting violent. A man lay bleeding near his mini-van full of supplies. A woman was screaming at the assailant. He paused in the act of unloading the van and promptly shot her in the head. The undead, responding to the gunfire, ambled in the direction of the shooter. Raven watched in horror as the desperate murderer was surrounded by the dead. He fired five shots, dropping five ghouls at his feet, and then in a last act of helpless desperation put the revolver in his mouth and blew his own brains out. In the end he gave his life for some bottled water, Budweiser and canned chili. She couldn't look away while he was consumed, piece by piece, by the teeming undead.

Raven's attention was drawn to more gunshots at the truck stop on the other side of the road. The good ole boy with the assault rifle bagged himself a couple more creatures. Clearly tensions were high at the Jackpot Fuel Depot.

The fact that the fire engine red bucket truck with the boom in the air stood out like a sore thumb in the empty parking lot worried Brook. Pretty soon the store across the road would be emptied and she was certain the Bi-Mart would be the next to be ransacked.

Carl planned to drop in and try to find a ladder so Brook wouldn't have to freefall to the floor. He got on his belly and thrust his legs through the broken skylight into open airspace. Slowly inching his legs into the void, he paused with his upper body still residing on the roof and counterbalancing the lower half of him. All he could think of was the scene in "Jaws" when the great white shark zeroed in on the swimmer's legs, only in his mind's eye it was a hungry zombie homing in on his exposed extremities.

He muttered under his breath, "Nothing ventured, nothing gained." And for good measure, "Higher power, don't fail me now."

Not wanting to prolong the suspense, he fully committed, hanging on with only his fingertips. Carl discovered that he was not as strong as he used to be. He was forced to let go. He and Brook had underestimated the distance; it was closer to fifteen feet from his toes to the floor. Thankfully he had chosen the window over the patio furniture section. His fall was broken by an outdoor chaise lounge with an overstuffed all weather mattress.

Chapter 25
Day 2 - Wahkeena Falls Parking Lot, Oregon

Ike was well aware of the dire situation he was in. He was in no position to be positive. He had seen so much death in person and on television these past two days he was beginning to numb to it.

Leo had tried to comfort him, but Ike put on a big man act and pushed him away.

After a few words in private, Cade and Rawley approached the feverish, shaking, young boy.

Cade spoke first. "Ike, I've only known you for a couple of days so I'm having a hard time deciding how to put this. Out of respect for you I have to be blunt. You are going to turn into one of them soon," he said, pointing at one of the unmoving corpses. "My question to you is, how do you want to handle it? You can do it by your own hand and on your own terms. Or if you want one of us to do it, or Leo....the choice is yours." Cade walked over to one of the picnic tables and sat down, his head hanging as he struggled with the enormity of the situation.

Everyone remained silent for a full five minutes.

The muffled rushing water of Wahkeena Falls was the only sound. If there hadn't been fourteen dead bodies, the stench of cordite and death hanging over the parking lot this splendid July day, it would have been a serene setting.

"Will I see Mom and Dad again?"

"Isaac Jerome Jackson, why do you think they dragged our butts to church every Sunday? There is a better place... and normal Mom and Dad will be there. Nana and Poppa will be with them waiting on us. You go check it out, I'll be close behind." Leo stopped breathing and held back tears before drawing in a deep breath and continuing, "I know that we will all be together soon."

The shaking was getting exponentially worse; Ike's skin glistened with sweat. Summoning the courage of ten men, he broke the silence and said, "I'll do it myself."

Not giving him time to rethink the monumental decision he had just made, Cade pulled his compact Glock 19 from the shoulder holster, removed the magazine, pulled the slide back to ensure there was one round of 9mm in the chamber and handed the pistol to him butt first.

Leo closed the distance and gave his brother a long drawn out hug.

Ike was failing fast and shaking uncontrollably. He pulled away from his brother, said a quiet tearful goodbye and disappeared around the front of the preschool bus.

It was barely ten seconds before the sharp report of the pistol made Leo start.

Cade walked purposefully around the bus. Ike had done it the right way; the back of his head was gone and there were powder burn marks around his lips. Death had been instantaneous. Ike was headed home.

Cade found beach towels inside the bus, retrieved one, and then out of respect covered the young boy's body. Then the men foraged for rocks to cover Ike's body with. They had little time to dig a grave, so this was the best they could do. The gorge had had a lot of volcanic activity in the past so it wasn't hard to find enough rocks to fully conceal his small frame.

Leo uttered his final goodbyes privately. "I love you bro. I'm sorry it had to happen to you. See you soon." He was sure to stack the last rock on his brother's makeshift grave.

With tears streaming down his face, Leo trudged to the Sequoia and slumped in the passenger seat.

Cade retrieved two lengths of hose and the two five-gallon plastic water containers from the truck and threw one of each to Rawley. They siphoned enough gas from the bus to fill both containers.

Cade placed one of the containers into the Sequoia and conferred with Rawley. "With this fuel, I think we can make Biggs Junction. We should get there before nightfall if I-84 isn't a parking lot."

"We probably ought to find some more containers and poach as much gas as we can along the way. We're driving a couple of thirsty rigs," Rawley said, nodding his head at the two SUVs.

Chapter 26
Day 2 - Whiteville, North Carolina

Carl sat as still as possible and let his eyes adjust to the semidarkness. While he listened for any movement or sound, his vivid imagination worked overtime. He was sure there were fifty undead waiting for him in the aisles. Although nothing had started moaning or taken a bite out of him yet, his guard was still up.

Having grown up in the 1970's, Carl remembered people ripping off gas in his neighborhood during Carter's glorious reign. A day wouldn't go by without a news story about someone getting their gas siphoned in the middle of the night. The garden aisle was five feet from where he had landed. Carl noticed the garden hose they would need if they were forced to siphon gas. He made a mental note to grab a length on the way out.

Brook looked down through the skylight at her brother. "Raven says there are a whole bunch of walkers coming out of the woods behind the store. Hurry up and find a ladder."

Every muscle screamed at him to stay seated, yet he hauled his big frame out of the comfortable chaise lounge and went in search of the tool aisle. Walking alone in the dark store without a flashlight made him feel very vulnerable. The hardware section was in the back right of the store. There were five aisles to search. Finally he found an aluminum extension ladder in the very last one. It was difficult manhandling the twelve feet of ladder to the middle of the store quietly. The last corner Carl rounded had a display of plant food canisters stacked pyramid like. The end of the ladder took out the bottom row and they noisily clattered around his feet. Carl almost lost his footing amidst the rolling containers. He managed to stay upright and stood the ladder on end. It made a lot of noise as he pulled it to its full twenty-two feet of extension. An even louder clang resonated when the ladder's end met the lip of the skylight. He braced the ladder for Brook while she descended. To his dismay, a faint moaning started somewhere in the store.

Raven sat statuelike on the rooftop surveying the scene. The back parking lot of the store now had several walkers ambling around with no real purpose. There was constant gunfire and commotion coming from the direction of the truck stop.

*****

When Brook reached the floor she delivered the bad news about the walking dead amassing outside. Carl hushed her and told her to listen for a minute. A muffled ghostly moan was coming from behind a closed door somewhere in the building. Cautiously the two started searching for the sporting goods section. As they set out, Carl pointed towards the garden hose; Brook gave him a nod and said, "On the way out."

Carl grabbed three large black nylon gym bags from the sporting good section. He kept two and threw one to Brook.

After a short search, Brook exclaimed quietly, "I've found the guns."

Carl helped her pick out two shotguns, a Mossberg 500 pump and a Remington 870 express camouflage model with a pistol grip. Carl removed the tags, found the slings and attached them to the weapons. Although he turned the place upside down there were no pistols to be had in the store. For good measure they also chose a hunting rifle. It was a Remington model 700 in .223 caliber fitted with a Leupold scope. They finished filling up two bags with twelve gauge shells, and all of the long rifle ammunition they could find. There were only three boxes of .223; they all went in the bag. Brook picked out a very sharp folding knife. They filled the third bag with canned food, beef jerky, peanuts and all of the bottled water it would hold.

The moans coming from whatever was trapped were now accompanied by a steady pounding. Carl shoved six of the twelve gauge slugs into the Model 500 and chambered a round. Brook loaded the other shotgun.

"Let's see where the sound is coming from," Carl said.

"I think we should get out of here," Brook countered.

"I want to take just one quick look. OK?"

"Fine," Brook said as she flicked open the pocket knife, "but make it quick. I'm going back up to the roof after I get a length of hose."

Carl followed the sound to its source. The noises were coming from behind a closed door with a two foot square glass window inset chest high. The sign on the door read "Loss Prevention-Employees Only." Inside was one of the infected. It wore a security guard's uniform and something had taken a big chunk of flesh from its neck. A good amount of dark dried blood blended in with the black rent-a-cop uniform. Carl tip toed forward and peered in the window. He could see that there were handcuffs and a pistol still on its hip.

The pale faced creature noticed Carl and started throwing itself at the door and window. The moaning from the undead thing rose in volume the second it set its lifeless glassy eyes on him.

Carl coveted the pistol on the ghoul's hip and he was determined to get it. When he tested the knob it turned freely. To his relief the dead bolt was not thrown. It was comforting to know the undead didn't remember how to open doors, or lock them. Slowly, shotgun at the ready, he turned the brushed steel knob and partially opened the door.

Carl guessed that the undead guard had been rotting in the stifling office for some time. The revolting odor made his eyes water. He composed himself after a few dry heaves. He slowly turned the doorknob, hoping to get the initiative on the imprisoned walker. The creature's strength caught him off guard. It shouldered the door open and came for him with arms outstretched, its fingers and mouth longing for his flesh. Carl misjudged the thing's speed; it grabbed ahold of his shirt pulling its gaping maw toward his exposed neck. Carl discharged the shotgun at close range. The walking corpse was blown backwards, pale bony fists still clutching fabric, its rib cage and left arm destroyed by the buckshot.

A new chorus of moans started up after the weapon's deafening discharge. Behind a second windowless door, another room still held undead. They started battering the door, flesh eating curiosity getting the best of them.

The guard didn't stay down; it worked itself back into a standing position. Carl racked another shell and took careful aim. The next blast separated the creature's head from its body. The zombie fell with a thud, blood sluicing from the cavity where its head used to be attached. It was a messy task turning the dead security guard over to access the weapon. The pistol turned out to be a Sig Sauer M&P .40 caliber and there were two spare magazines on the belt. He took the gun, belt and all.

With each new blow the back door started to splinter. An arm punched through the hollow wood veneer door and felt around for prey before withdrawing back into the hole. A pale milky white face filled the jagged opening. Carl felt devoured by the dead eyes lusting for his flesh. He knew it was only a matter of time before the door would totally give way. Instead of shooting the ghoul in the face with the shotgun and further eroding the door's structural integrity, he turned and moved as fast as his forty-five year old legs would propel him. Climbing up the ladder would be difficult as loaded down as he was, but they needed all of the goodies he was carrying.

Carl looked up and was greeted by two familiar faces. Slinging the Mossberg over his shoulder he started lugging the heavy duffel bags up the aluminum rungs.

A tremendous crash came from the rear of the Bi-Mart. The dead had finally breached the flimsy door and were coming for him.

Brook and Raven saw them first. The uniformed ghouls were heading right for Carl's outstretched legs. The first ghoul slipped and fell on the same canisters of plant fertilizer that had nearly tripped up Carl, followed by its fellows. The tin can obstacle course slowed their pursuit enough for Carl to chuck the heavy bags up onto the roof. After clumsily regaining their footing, the creatures, mouths open and loudly moaning, threw their rotten bodies at the base of the fully extended ladder.

Brook's straining fingers brushed Carl's just before the ladder was knocked from the lip of the skylight. He barely managed to grab hold as gravity fully took over and stole the ladder. He was strong enough to momentarily hang suspended, but the glass still in the frame was shredding his bare hands. Compared to the fate that hungrily waited down below him, not being able to high five for a month was worth the tradeoff.

Brook thought quickly, then held on to Raven's legs and anchored her. She lowered her through the skylight until she hung, suspended upside down. Raven stretched along the length of her uncle's body, trying to snare the shotgun's sling.

"I've got it. Pull me up!" Raven yelled out.

Feet planted on the skylight frame, Brook hauled all sixty pounds of her daughter, the shotgun sling firmly clasped in her hands, back to safety. They both held onto the thin nylon strap encircling Carl's upper body. Brook's muscles cramped and her body quivered while she fought to belay Carl's weight. Raven's grip was tenuous at best. Brook implored her brother to pull with all of his might.

Carl looked down at the undead mosh pit below his dangling feet and summoned every last ounce of strength from his tired arms and shoulders. With help from the girls, he was able to hook a leg over and fully pull himself onto the roof. Carl lay there, flat on his back, gasping for breath and stared thankfully up at the brilliant blue sky.

When he had his wind back and could command his quivering legs to support him, he stood and stumbled after Brook and Raven.

Raven was the first to reach the roof's edge directly above the bucket truck. She surveyed the parking lot and said in a near whisper, "We have a problem."

Carl and Brook couldn't believe their eyes when they peered over the parapet.

Chapter 27
Day 2 - Bonneville, Oregon

Rawley noticed the headlights winking in the rearview mirror when he slowed to round a sharp curve in the road. A big grin crossed his face as it registered in his one track mind that the vehicle flashing him was the red Cabriolet driven by the two blonde beauties from the Vista House. Following them was the bright yellow Camaro and bringing up the rear was a lifted 4x4 pickup.

"Slow down, we have company," Rawley's voice came through the two-way radio resting on the console by Cade's Glock 19.

Leo relayed Cade's response into the Motorola. "Driver man says the next chance he gets he'll pull over."

Five minutes later they stopped on the off-ramp merging the old scenic highway with the interstate.

*****

The girls were warmly greeted by Rawley.

Cade cautiously walked towards the Dodge pickup to meet the driver, M4 carbine hanging from his body, locked and loaded.

"Howdy, how's it going, friend?" the man sitting in the truck asked, his voice accented with a Southern drawl.

One look and Cade knew that the older man could handle himself; he locked eyes and held Cade's gaze, and he exuded an air of self-confidence, usually evident in law enforcement or military men.

"Well, considering that the dead are walking around and I'm not one of them, pretty damn good! And you?" Cade said.

"Pardon my poor manners, name's Duncan Winters," the man said, extending his hand.

Cade met him halfway and returned the man's firm handshake.

"How did you end up travelling with the old man and the twins?"

"I was trying to get onto 84. I was aimin' to head east to Utah and find my brother. Before I got onto the off-ramp I saw a group of unarmed people murdered in cold blood. One big sumbitch of a biker gutted a little girl while I watched," Duncan said, his voice wavering.

"Was there a state cop present?"

"He was the first to die," Duncan said.

"Did anyone resist?" Cade probed for more info.

"No, they were butchered before they could do a thing. Whole mess lasted less than it takes to watch a commercial on the TV. Those pukes make the Viet Cong look like pacifists."

"Sounds like there was nothing you could have done to change the outcome by yourself," Cade said, trying to assuage the guilt that he detected.

"I felt a feeling of helplessness descend on me. I watched that madman and his boys have their way with those people, and after they murdered all of the men, they took the rest of the women with them."

Duncan stared into Cade's eyes, his rage evident, and said with a hard edge to his words, "At any cost, I'd like to send those pieces of shit to hell."

Cade had only two words to add, "I concur."

"I've got kin near Salt Lake City that I'd like to check up on. I was headed that way when this madness started. Maybe we can help each other until we part ways? Anyway, what I'm getting at is I'd like to roll with you all." Duncan waited patiently for an answer.

"There is something to be said for strength in numbers, but in all honesty my first priority is to get back East and find my wife and little girl. If we should run into the gang on the way, well, we will just have to cross that bridge when we get there."

"Guess I will take that as an affirmative, sir. I'll bring up the rear of the convoy and keep my eyes on our six."

"Settled then, we're oscar mike in five minutes," Cade said to the fellow ex-soldier.

Cade walked the line of vehicles and touched bases with Harry and the twins, then pulled Rawley away from the latter. Addressing Rawley, he explained, "I still intend on finding my family, but I want to make sure those animals don't kill any more people. So keep your eyes peeled; if we see them, we need to hit them hard and fast. No mercy."

"I'm with you brother," Rawley agreed.

*****

The convoy entered I-84 and snaked east single file. The Columbia River flew by on their left. As the day wore on the stifling heat made travel miserable. The hot gusting east wind only added to their misery. They had to stop a handful of times to siphon gas and to allow for restroom breaks.

Some stretches of the road were fully blocked by cars and trucks that needed to be pushed out of the way. They learned to use utmost caution when approaching vehicles on foot. A good number of the infected had died and then reanimated in their cars, effectively trapping them inside, where they waited patiently and quietly for anything to get near enough to attack.

The group stopped near the Bridge of the Gods to search a large multivehicle pileup and obtain more gas. Leo and Harry had volunteered to be the "suckers" as they had jokingly started to call themselves. Leo had almost met the same fate as his brother; he was siphoning gas from a Toyota Prius when a partially paralyzed crawler silently pulled itself along the road towards him. The creature knocked over the empty plastic gas cans waiting to be filled. The cans tumbled and clattered on the blacktop. Luck was on Leo's side, as the warning allowed enough time for him to crabwalk backwards on all fours and put some distance between himself and the ghoul. The young boy had probably been eight or nine when he died in the accident. The child zombie was naked save a pair of tattered Spiderman underwear and a shredded short sleeve shirt, reddish black with dried blood. The toothless face looked like it belonged to a meth addict; death had not been kind to him. The coarse rocky asphalt had been unforgiving as the ghoul strained to traverse it. Except for the head, the rest of his body looked like raw hamburger. Bite marks and missing flesh peppered its torso. The undead boy's mouth opened and closed but no sound emitted. Without mercy or second thought Leo drew the compact Glock and said, "Better you than me fucker," and put a bullet in the crawler's brain. He found that he was growing very thick skin after all he had been through. Being callous towards the undead wasn't necessarily a bad thing, because empathy didn't compliment survival. Leo followed the bloody slug track back to its source, it ended near a wrecked Camry. The crushed man and woman, who most likely used to be the boy's parents, had been killed in the wreck and remained dead. In the back next to the booster seat was a Gameboy with a bag full of cartridges. *I'll take that,* Leo thought as he scooped them up.

*****

They drove for hours without incident until they were forced to stop near the Oregon-Idaho border. A large group of infected blocked the road and then promptly swarmed the stopped caravan. The convoy reversed and turned around to get some road between them and the infected. Cade, Rawley and Duncan armed themselves, dismounted and strode towards the undead.

More of the ghouls piled clumsily out of a Casino shuttle van. Most had been baby boomers in their fifties and sixties. Rawley watched Cade as he moved with the grace of a big cat on the hunt. His M4 shouldered, he walked towards the undead in a combat crouch and fired single shots methodically into the walkers' heads. The steady rhythmic shooting, interspersed with the tinkling of the spent cartridges bouncing on the blacktop, shattered the quiet on the calm deserted highway. Seventeen undead had emerged from the Casino coach; they were covered with bite wounds and shredded flesh from the carnage they had endured while trapped inside. All of them now lay in a heap in front of Cade. Rawley, Leo and Duncan made quick work of the other walkers blocking the road.

Leo was especially proud to bag his first upright walker. The crawling boy hadn't given him room for concern, but the taller undead man was a different story. Leo was very nervous. His hands shook, nearly causing him to miss the close range shot. The Glock 19 held seventeen rounds. It took him six shots to finally drop the ghoul with a bullet to the brain. The undead bus driver fell to the pavement, sticky black matter dribbling from the dime-sized entry wound on his forehead.

*****

After nearly singlehandedly dispatching the creatures from the Coachman, Cade cautiously stepped inside the bus. He contemplated having one of the others drive it, but ruled it out because the gore splashed interior was a definite bio-hazard.

The survivors were fatigued and jittery from the constant adrenaline highs and lows and needed a break. After a brief period of uneasy rest, the decision was made to continue on. Everyone mounted up and the small convoy went off in search of an easily defensible place to stop for the night.

*****

Just across the border in Idaho they passed over a flat cement bridge spanning the Snake River. Cade slowed the Sequoia, exited the interstate and parked at the rest stop. The other vehicles followed suit. Everyone got out, stretched their legs and made small talk.

Portland was more than four hundred miles and ten hours away. They had made pretty good time considering the world had been turned upside down.

*****

Cade and Rawley were engaged in a strategy session when the screaming started from the direction of the restrooms. A group of undead had gotten trapped in the women's side of the small structure. Shelly pushed the door open and inadvertently stumbled right into their midst. The doorway was narrow, and allowed only one of the twins to escape. Shelly was not so fortunate. Cold bloody fingers intertwined with her long blond hair, and another pair of hands clamped around her left arm. The combined weight of the two bodies pulled her down. She was pounced on by a Troop of undead Girl Scouts. One zombie tore Shelly's hair from her head, effectively scalping her. She screamed until her voice box was torn from her neck. The remaining undead tumbled over the writhing pile on the ground and began pursuing Sheila.

Duncan proved himself adept with the stubby combat 12 gauge he kept displayed on the gun rack in his pickup. He only needed one shot each to drop the four bloated walking corpses.

"You fuckers…no…no…no!" each word from Rawley rose higher in octave while he ran to help the twins. He sprinted between Harry and the hysterical Sheila, SKS at the ready, and at point blank range shot both of the monsters that were eating Shelly.

Sheila shrieked her dead sister's name repeatedly. With the grim knowledge that Shelly would soon reanimate, Cade gently escorted Sheila to the other end of the rest area, hoping to spare her any more trauma.

Rawley held vigil over Shelly's corpse, praying to God that she wouldn't reanimate. Coppery smelling blood flowed from her shredded neck across the white tile floor, finally ending its journey at the drain. In a matter of minutes the inevitable started to happen. First her hand twitched and then her head moved side to side. Her eyelids opened revealing milky orbs. Rawley put the rifle to his shoulder; the single shot rang out, echoing off of the bathroom walls. Save for the gusting desert wind, the rest stop went quiet.

*****

Sheila wanted some time by herself, so Cade left her alone in his truck and sat on top of a picnic table deep in thought. He mourned the loss of Ike and Shelly. He reflected on how much he missed his family and said a silent prayer for them. Cade mulled over this latest encounter and subsequent loss and pondered how it would affect his travelling companions' morale. *Man, Rawley is going to need a shrink… if there are any still alive.*

*****

Cade was awed by the new guy's prowess with the shotgun; he got up off of the bench and sought out Duncan so they could get better acquainted. Duncan reluctantly shared his story.

He became adept at shooting during his first tour in Nam. While many of his fellow soldiers slept the day away or partied between patrols outside of the wire, he spent his spare time shooting on the government's dime. Eventually he befriended the Company armorer and soaked up all of the weapons knowledge he could.

When he was actually earning his paycheck, he flew slicks. That's what the men in the 1st Air Calvary called the UH-1 Huey. It was the helicopter workhorse of the war and he flew them all over Vietnam, Laos and Cambodia. His Huey had ferried some of the last people out of Saigon after it fell in 1975, and then after landing on the pitching deck of an aircraft carrier, to make room for other landing helos he helped the deck crewmen push his baby off into the roiling South China sea.

Cade reciprocated with his own story, but for now he left out all of the Delta Team black-ops stuff. He touched over his tours in both theaters in the sandbox as a Ranger with the 75th. It was the perfect time to bring up something that had been nagging him.

"I need to be frank with you Duncan. It was fully on me to check and clear the bathrooms. I didn't even notice the extra vehicle. I let a kid down this morning, and it led to his death."

"I'm an old man but this ain't my first rodeo, son. Don't beat yourself up. You're used to being in the field with swinging dicks that know how to take care of themselves. This mother hen thing is gonna take some getting used to."

"It still doesn't make it any easier..." Cade said, his voice going quiet.

"Nothing worth doing is. I got your back, soldier. If it helps any, from now on we can both babysit."

Cade thanked the fellow soldier and got up to go walk the perimeter of the rest stop. Duncan traipsed back to the rest of the survivors.

*****

Rawley inspected the dead. Five of the six were young teen girls and the other was old enough to be their mom. How they all ended up in the bathroom together was a mystery until Leo made the observation that the door only opened one way, inward. Some of the girls had defensive wounds on their hands and some had been fed on before they reanimated. The den mother's neck and blouse were caked with dried blood and it appeared she was the first to turn before attacking the others.

*****

When Cade returned from his walk around the rest area he helped the others move the dead downwind from the vehicles. There was no way to bury Shelly; the ground was rock solid. They settled on a brief service before moving her near some colorful desert flowers growing on the periphery of the green-brown grass. Sheila cried through the kind words the others had to say. Rawley was visibly upset; he had taken a liking to Shelly the moment they first met.

115

They tried to keep themselves busy. It helped to keep their minds off of the fallen. The mood around the rest area was solemn and dark.

*****

Harry extracted nearly a full tank of gas from the minivan while Leo broke the rear window. Leo's nose was instantly assailed by the sickening sweet smell coming from the two dead lapdogs on the front seats.

Camping gear, Girl Scout books, uniforms and literature, plus a cooler full of warm water and spoiled food was arranged in an orderly fashion in the back of the stifling van. Leo and Harry pulled all of the gear out of the minivan and spread it out on the still warm asphalt. It looked like they were having a yard sale. They took the water purifier, binoculars, tent and six sleeping bags. They were sure to come in handy since it would be getting dark soon and the nights were very cold in the high desert.

*****

Cade called the group over to one of the picnic benches in the middle of the grass.

"I think this would be a good place to stay the night. It's off the road far enough, defensible, and the freeway is straight in both directions. We are in the open but at least we'll hear and see any approaching vehicles before they're upon us."

"We could circle the vehicles like a wagon train and anyone wanting to sleep under the stars could sleep in the center. I will volunteer for guard duty," Harry offered.

"Not a good idea Harry… we're not camping, we're trying to survive in a hostile environment. The vehicles would offer better shelter from the elements, animals and *those* things; but if *you* want to sleep under the stars, I'm not going to try stop you."

Harry left the meeting in a huff. Constructive criticism it was not. He felt talked down to and belittled. *Why did I even tag along with these ungrateful whelps anyway?*

*****

"Leo. You want to pull guard duty first?" Cade asked, trying to include him. He had been withdrawn and quiet since the death of his brother Ike, even more so now that they had lost Shelly.

"I will if I can borrow the smaller pistol."

"You can have the Glock until we find a place to acquire some more weapons."

Cade removed the gun and an extra magazine from the holster and handed them to the young man.

"Don't forget, the safety is on the trigger, and always assume the gun is loaded."

"I promise I'll only shoot at those fuckin' creatures."

"Happy hunting," Cade said, admiring Leo's new found bravado.

Chapter 28
Day 2 - Whiteville, North Carolina

Carl quickly stole a glance over the three foot wall surrounding the rooftop. It was the stench his brain registered first. The smell of death clung to everything; it was something Carl knew he would never get used to. At least thirty of the undead were shuffling about the parking lot. Several had taken an interest in the truck. The bucket was at eye level, right in front of his face, but he didn't dare do anything until he had a moment to collect his thoughts.

"Where did they all come from?" he asked Brook.

"Raven told me they came through the trees over there," she responded, pointing at the thicket of dogwoods.

"I think they're workers from that factory near the interstate," Raven offered.

The parking lot in front of the metal prefab building was full of cars. Quite a few of the walkers did have on work type clothes, coveralls, aprons, work boots and such. Most of them were slightly overweight men, and their movement was quite lethargic. Even though the walkers moved slower than a living person, you still had to be careful not to develop a false sense of security. The dead had the overwhelming strength in numbers, therefore a seemingly safe situation could turn deadly in a heartbeat.

Carl said, "Just great! This is the biggest gathering of these things I have seen in one place and they just *haaadd* to show up while we are cooling our heels on a Bi-Mart roof."

Raven, always willing to point out the facts, added her two cents. "Don't forget Uncle Carl, our only means of transportation happens to be sitting down there, fully surrounded by them."

As they watched, twenty more undead filtered through the trees. "We need to make a run for it. I suspect that the swing shift must have just ended," Carl said, failing in his attempt to be funny.

"There is a time and place..." Brook was abruptly cut off by a massive explosion at the Jackpot fuel mart.

The shockwave rolled over their heads, followed by intense heat and overpressure caused by the displaced air. It made their ears hurt, causing a prolonged ringing. The blast lasted only a few seconds. It felt like an invisible hand had slapped them completely flat on the rooftop. The surface felt cool on Brook's stomach as the heat wave rolled over her back. She put her arm around Raven's head and shoulders to shield her.

Most of their exposed arm hair had been singed; the awful smell still mingled with the zombies' stench. Debris rained down around them, sounding and feeling like an intense hailstorm. A severed human arm, still wearing a bulky diver's watch, landed with a thud near Carl's head. He removed the indestructible Timex Ironman, murmuring, "You won't need that anymore." *Finally a little truth in advertising*, Carl thought.

Carl wanted to go see what had caused the explosion but didn't want to waste the diversion it afforded them. Once again he thanked the Big Guy above.

Carl looked down at the stinking mass of hungry zombies. "Some of them are going around the building towards the gas station. I'm going to try to get inside the truck."

Dangling the keys in his direction, Brook pointed out, "You'll need these."

Carl pocketed the keys. "When I start down the boom I want you two to get in the bucket and keep out of their sight."

"Big brother... *be careful.*"

Carl scaled over the wall, momentarily paused inside the bucket, and then climbed onto the boom, feet first with his head looking down the wall at the asphalt below.

The zombies noticed and were moaning and reaching up towards him. He felt like a canary in a cage with the big fat tomcat hungrily staring at him.

Carl took a handful of thick black grease from the hydraulic piston by his head and swabbed a liberal amount under his nose. It had a harsh chemical odor, but anything was better than the stink of the walking dead.

Here goes nothing. Inch by inch Carl lowered himself towards the relative safety of the truck's bed.

*****

Brook looped the duffle bags' straps around a piece of metal protruding from the bucket and then stepped into the confined space. Thank God Raven was as small as she was, because it was getting cozy in the fiberglass bucket. Brook held her daughter, trying her best to calm her. Raven was shaking uncontrollably; she had been through ten lifetime's worth of trauma in one day. Brook feared her daughter was going to have severe PTSD if they somehow found a way to stay alive.

Carl had shimmied a third of the way down the boom, but he was still a good distance from the cab. The shotgun, hanging from his shoulder, banged steadily against the boom, alerting the entire undead crowd to his presence. The massed ghouls were agitated and more were arriving. Below him the moaning intensified.

The flesh-eaters were now three deep around the truck. Their sheer numbers were causing it to rock like a boat at sea. Brook struggled to keep Raven calm in the swaying bucket.

Three immolated undead staggered around the corner and headed for the utility truck, oblivious to the fact that they were on fire. Carl didn't want the walking torches to get anywhere near the truck's fuel tanks and he really had no desire to end up crispy like them. To his relief, after a few more ungainly steps the charbroiled trio fell short and ceased moving.

We almost had a Waco moment there. Carl had no idea why they seized up, he was just grateful they did. Shooting three moving corpses from his position would have been nearly impossible. His best guess was that their brains must have cooked in their skulls.

Six feet separated Carl from the clamoring crowd of undead; the grease under his nose was no match for the disgusting odor radiating from them. He had chosen the shorter of the two shotguns and had six shells loaded into the tube under the barrel. The truck's rear window was near enough that he had to choose which side of the bed he wanted to land on. The driver's side had a few less walkers; the ones on the right were so thick they were starting to crawl on top of each other, getting close to boarding the truck. Carl knew if he didn't move hastily he was going to be dinner.

A formerly teenaged zombie wriggled up onto the passenger side of the truck and grabbed for him. Carl placed the Mossberg muzzle three inches from the ghoul's upper lip. Her undead eyes showed no hint of recognition that her time on earth was over. Hundreds of lead pellets disintegrated her face from the nose up. A new zombie emerged, coated with the other's brains and exhibiting the same mindless drive. Carl crouched down, racked the slide, and aimed the shotgun at the truck's back window. The blast imploded the window. From the angle of the shot and where he was laying he failed to anticipate what happened next. Buckshot and sharp shards of glass ricocheted back, peppering his face. Somehow his sight was spared.

After wiping the blood from his eyes, he wedged his big frame through the opening, just escaping the reach of the persistent ghoul and its hungry mouth full of yellowed teeth. Lying on the bench seat was an awkward position for a man of his size. Getting the key into the ignition was going to be a pain in the ass, let alone trying to drive the truck like a contortionist. More zombies had managed to get onto the back of the truck and were reaching their dirty rotting hands through the shattered opening.

The engine started on the first try. Carl manipulated the tree mounted shifter into reverse and pushed on the gas pedal with his hand. The truck accelerated backwards from the store. Wrenching the steering wheel all the way to the left, he gave it more gas.

Brook had kept her head down throughout the gunfire but now that the truck was moving she risked a look. An audible gasp escaped her mouth when she saw the surrounding army of ghouls. To her horror, she saw that three of the creatures had found their way onto the rear of the truck and were trying to enter the cab through the broken rear window.

Brook chose the Remington over the Ithaca, it was heavier but it held four more shells. She racked a round into the chamber and clicked the safety off. While bouncing up and down in the bucket, Brook lined up the iron sight on the front of the shotgun and pulled the trigger. The buckshot peppered the ghouls around their heads, but did no real damage. Several walkers were sucked under the dual rear wheels and caused the bucket to violently bob up and down. Brook felt the truck start to list. The weight of the fully extended bucket had changed the truck's center of gravity. She jammed the lever all the way down to the detent. The boom started to retract and slowly lower at once. Brook's quick thinking once again saved them all.

The two undead had gotten stuck in a dangerous place on the truck and they didn't know how to work their way out. While they feebly struggled the enormous boom folded down on top of them and settled into its resting place. The weight of the cherry picker caused their internal organs to explode; bodily fluids coated the truck bed. The bigger one was crushed into a fetal position, its gasses escaping with a loud farting noise. The other's fate was no better. The wide boom acted like a pile driver and pushed down on its head, pinning it to the diamond plate decking.

Carl had his hands full, blindly driving the big truck from the floorboards, while a cold clammy hand continued to claw at him. In addition to all of the superficial cuts on his face and scalp, the ghoul's jagged dirty fingernails were gouging deep furrows into his back.

Brook was practically hanging upside down from the bucket when it finally stopped its downward movement. The remaining creature found itself trapped; it appeared to be doing the breast stroke, its pale torso half in and out of the shattered rear window. She calmly put the shotgun on the zombie's exposed neck; the blast decapitated the monster, its severed head falling from the truck and bouncing multiple times on the hard blacktop.

Brook noted the two squirming carcasses lodged under the lift boom. Crouching low and getting to eye level, she was astounded at how hopeless their situation was, yet they still strained and snapped trying to bite her. She racked another round into the shotgun and placed the barrel flush with the ghoul's temple. One shot stilled it. The other monster's head was stuck farther under the hydraulic piston that actuated the up and down movement of the arm. There was no way to safely get a headshot without damaging the hydraulic lines that snaked nearby. After chambering another shell, she buried the gun deep into the creature's crushed chest cavity, all the way up to the trigger guard, the muzzle lodged in the ghoul's throat. The report was much quieter than she had anticipated, but resulted in a disgusting shower of gray brain matter, blood and spinal fluid. The trapped zombie shuddered once and then went limp.

"That was the last of the bastards on the truck, but we're still surrounded!" Brook exclaimed as Carl's bloody head popped into view. He took in the destruction the big truck had caused. At least twenty of the zombies were pasted to the blacktop unmoving; many more were severely injured or reduced to crawling half-corpses, their arms propelling them after the red bucket truck. The truck looped the parking lot; nearly fifty of the flesh-eaters stiffly marched after. The explosion and resulting inferno at the truck stop beckoned the dead from the factory like moths to a bug zapper.

Carl aimed the vehicle towards the path of least resistance. Only three walkers were between them and the open road. The young girl zombie went under the front of the truck as if sucked into a vacuum. The other two were male; they both had fresh bloody wounds. It was a perfect 7-10 split. Carl sideswiped the one in a business suit and threw him into a parked Hyundai. The utility truck clipped the last walker and sent the putrid pedestrian rolling into the gutter with multiple compound fractures jutting from its flesh.

The truck jumped the curb swaying left and right, straightened out and then raced from the corpse-strewn parking lot. The brake lights flashed as it slowed momentarily and then rounded the corner disappearing from sight. The crowd of zombies moaned as if in disappointment but kept hobbling after.

Through it all, Raven had stayed curled up on the floor of the bucket sobbing. It was all that could be expected of an eleven-year-old under such duress.

Chapter 29
Day 2 - District of Columbia

The two HH-60G Pave Hawks of the 160th SOAR crossed the Potomac River and slowed to 60 knots. The Night Stalkers piloted their helicopter's NOE (nap-of-the-earth), hugging the ground's contour while running dark the three hundred twenty-five miles from Fort Bragg. As they neared the target the two Apache gunships gained altitude and started a racetrack pattern. Reaper Three and Four would provide over watch for the hovering Black Hawks as the Delta Teams were inserted.

Mike Desantos had never asked his men to accept a mission he wasn't willing to undertake himself, especially with this much at stake. He looked at his men and then looked at the darkened city through the port side window. There were no streetlights. All of the buildings looked cold and uninviting. Multiple fires reflected a red orange glow off of the river, making it look like misplaced lava. Mike saw the masses of undead lurching about the city streets, illuminated by the firelight cast from the burning buildings.

The pilot gave a thumbs up and then held his hand open, fingers spread. The silent signal let Mike know they were five minutes from the target.

Captain Mike Desantos was the 18a detachment Commander and his 180a Warrant Officer, number two man, was Deke Clifton. Mike would be leading his Delta team, call sign Zulu-One. The six operators would fast rope from the helicopter onto the west roof of the target. Deke's team of six Delta operators, Zulu-Two, would insert on the east rooftop.

The Special-Ops pilot held the bird in a perfect, steady hover as the six operators, led by Mike, fast roped two at a time from the helo's open doors onto the roof. The night vision goggles adorning their faces rendered the scene in a green glow. Litter and bodies were strewn across the expansive lawn. A large helicopter sat quiet in the grass; next to it zombies were feeding on the body of a Marine in full dress blues, his white and black brimmed hat lying by his eviscerated body. The ghouls paused briefly and stared intently at the insertion taking place.

All of the men were safely on the roof. The pair of Pave Hawks, having deposited their human cargo, accelerated quickly out of sight. The undead, having lost interest, resumed consuming the fallen Marine's body.

*****

Mike had been inside this building before as a guest. This time he would be breaking and entering.

Sergeant Darwin Maddox anchored a thick nylon rope onto the sturdy steel bracket that secured the rooftop air scrubbers servicing the building. Silenced H&K MP7A1 at the ready, he pushed off with his back to the open air and smoothly rappelled over the edge, landing on the portico below. He went to one knee and scanned the area with his NVGs, carbine moving as one with his eyes.

Speaking in a whisper, Maddox called "Clear," his throat mic amplifying the words and transmitting them through all of the team's earpieces. Brent, Haskell and Calvin joined Maddox on the terrace. A moment later Desantos and Clark formed up; all six men were together in the alcove a mere ten feet above where the zombies roamed.

Maddox expertly applied the DET cord around the secure door frame and prepared the charge. The men turned their heads away when the cord detonated so their NV goggles wouldn't wash out, momentarily blinding them. The explosion wasn't spectacular. A low rumble and a puff of smoke later the door fell inward and landed with a muffled thud on the thick navy blue carpet. The smell of death wafting from within didn't surprise Mike.

The six men stacked up hand on shoulder, weapons at the ready and entered the glowing green room, barrels covering their zone. The room was uninhabited, but the scene was surreal. A wide mahogany antique desk, made with wood sourced from the HMS Resolute, sat facing their breach point. A secure phone and a computer with two large LCD screens shared space with family photos on the expansive desktop. The American flag was prominently displayed on the left side of the desk. On the opposite was a flag bearing the presidential seal. They were in the Oval Office of the White House without an invitation.

They stood still and listened for sound or movement. They were greeted with silence.

Mike turned the knob and slowly eased the solid walnut door open, his carbine sweeping left to right. An empty hall was revealed in the green glow of his NVGs. He communicated with his men using only hand signals. Each operator had a flashing IR strobe affixed to the back of his tactical helmet, only visible through night vision optics.

Once again the men stacked up to enter the hall. Their silenced weapons emitted green IR beams that danced in the air. It was like being at a laser light show without the blaring Pink Floyd. The hallway was clear. The men moved in single file, spaced a few feet apart. Sergeant Clark watched their six while a stern looking portrait of George Washington watched them all as they padded down the hall, weapons and beams sweeping the corridor.

The White House was very secure with blast and bullet proof windows and doors. It lent for a very quiet interior. They detected scratchy moans coming from somewhere in the West Wing. Captain Desantos was on point; he was the one that noticed the bloody hand prints first. He feared the worst. POTUS had two little daughters and these happened to be too small to be left by an adult. A blood trail meandered down the hallway through a set of closed, ornately carved double doors. Mike's earpiece came alive with the voice of Zulu-Two's team leader, Deke Clifton.

"This is Rainman, how copy?"

"Cowboy here, sit rep?"

"We made contact with multiple infected, Sergeant Wholford is WIA (wounded in action). He has been infected."

"Copy that. Secure your casualty and proceed to objective."

*****

In the East Wing of the White House, the infected Sergeant agreed to take his life before he could turn and jeopardize the mission. Deke handed the man a blister packet containing one gel caplet. Sergeant Wholford opened the package and promptly swallowed the pill. He sat down and was relieved of his weapons. His eyes closed and his body convulsed; he was dead seconds later. As commanding Officer, it was Deke's responsibility to make sure the man stayed dead. Two rounds from his silenced MP7 assured Wholford would not reanimate.

The entire Zulu-One Delta Team stood in front of the doors while their leader received a situation report from the other team. Mike had committed the floor plan to memory. They were nearing the president's Chief of Staff Emanuel Jones' personal office.

Mike's team made their first contact near the end of the blood-tracked hallway. The two zombies staggered out of the Chief of Staff's office. Undead didn't have good night vision; the Chief of Staff caromed off of an elaborately carved table and fumbled his way towards the Delta Team. An IR beam painted the walker's face; in the eerie green glow of Mike's NV goggles he concluded it was in fact the President's right hand man, Emanuel Jones. The guttural sound that escaped from its mouth confirmed the worst: high ranking members had indeed returned with the President as intelligence had suggested. Unfortunately the infection had spread inside the most secure residence in the free world.

Mike took careful aim. The silenced H&K MP7 coughed twice; the two bullets entered the zombie's forehead high and opened the top of its head spraying flecks of bone and brain all over the beautiful oil paintings adorning the walls. Another ghoul ambled out of the office; the woman had bite wounds all over her torso. The young intern had seen better days. She was minus all of her internal organs and both arms had been partially consumed. It was apparent she had lost a lot of blood before she died; her entire lower body was crimson red.

Mike sidestepped Emanuel Jones' body and calmly put a bullet into the intern's temple just behind the left eye. The projectile scrambled her brains and she dropped instantly.

Mike entered the office and called out "Clear" a moment later. Once he was back in the hallway he produced a small digital camera from his thigh pocket and recorded the faces of the undead for later confirmation.

"Cowboy, this is Rainman, we are outside of POTUS's master bedroom, preparing for entry."

"Copy that. Proceed at will," Mike answered.

*****

The remaining five shooters led by Warrant Officer Deke Clifton breached the door with DET cord. The room was in shambles and the walls were blood streaked. Broken furniture lay strewn about.

Suddenly two small figures emerged from the dark grand master bathroom. Deke had been briefed before the mission and had studied and memorized the faces of all of the VIPs in the White House. Even tinted green he recognized the President's young daughters rushing at him, so he held his fire. When he realized that the children were zombies he engaged them with his silenced weapon. The girls were faster than any other undead that he had encountered. Carly, the youngest, leapt at him like a feral cat. He shot from the hip, and the un-aimed bullets went left and high. His fate was sealed when she latched her teeth onto his forearm and held on. Her body weight caused him to swing around towards his team while inadvertently discharging his weapon. Sergeant Dean Matthews caught two through the neck a millisecond before Sergeant Lowery was gut shot below his body armor. The next two operators in the stack, Rooks and Dooley, were unscathed; they promptly rushed forward to help. Sergeant First Class Lopez who was bringing up the rear was saved by his bulletproof vest; the two errant bullets still had enough punch to knock him down. The other child zombie latched onto Sergeant Lowery's neck near his jugular. The little creature shook her head and came away with a prize.

Lopez, still on the floor, aimed through the holographic sight on his MP7; the feeding zombie looked up and hissed at him. A three round burst from his weapon rendered her face unrecognizable.

Deke couldn't believe it. He was fatally injured by the smallest superficial bite; tiny teeth marks were visible on the exposed flesh between his gloved hand and his ACU sleeve. He let his weapon hang from its sling and checked Matthews' pulse. It was too late for him. The young operator had bled out already and was starting to turn a pallid gray. The carpet was slick with blood and the gut shot Lowery was fighting to breathe, bloody air bubbles frothing from his mouth. Acrid cordite, comingling with the metallic smell of blood, filled the Presidential Suite.

Deke tended to the rapidly fading Lowery. Lopez was smarting from the bullets his vest had absorbed. He gingerly moved forward to assist Deke just as Lowery reanimated and rolled over onto his stomach. Deke stood erect, backpedaled and put a plush chair between him and the corpse. The creature that was once Lowery managed to rise, allowing the entire contents of his bowels to spill through the gaping entry wounds. Fecal odor now permeated the room. Lopez gagged as he double-tapped his undead teammate with his silenced carbine.

A dry rattling moan originated from the next room. Lopez entered the adjoining marble tiled bathroom, in a combat crouch, with his carbine at the ready. The sound was coming from the white clawfoot tub. He approached cautiously and looked over the edge at what remained of the First Lady's body. She was naked and twitching in the bottom of the empty vessel. It appeared she had been attacked and eaten by her undead children. The bite marks were small, but so much of her had been consumed the only thing she could do was track movement with her eyes and click her jaws open and closed.

Lopez, Rooks and Dooley finished clearing the President's private residence. Lopez called out, "Clear."

Deke hailed Mike.

"This is Rainman, I've been infected. Wholford, Matthews and Lowery are all KIA, Lopez is assuming command of Zulu-Two, how copy?"

*****

On the other side of the White House Mike halted in his tracks, let his weapon hang on its sling, and rubbed his temples before answering.

"Cowboy, copy that. What the hell happened?"

Deke recounted how he had paused briefly before engaging the First children. "Shit went FUBAR on me. I take full responsibility. FLOTUS is dead. I repeat the First Lady is down."

Lopez took command of Zulu-Two and ordered his men to digitally document the scene and retrieve DNA swabs from all of the dead. Rooks took the camera from Deke and captured images of the dead girls and the First Lady, who was still hungrily eyeing the soldiers.

Deke confirmed his pistol was loaded by pulling the slide back far enough to see brass in the chamber; he then stepped to the undead Mrs. Odero and fired one bullet into her brain. He started to shake, not only from what he had just done, but also from the viral process taking place throughout his entire body. Deke's limbs were going numb. The last time he felt this miserable was during the cold water survival course at Fort Benning so many years ago. He had survived that day but he knew he wasn't finishing this one. The weary soldier closed the door behind him and pulled the photo of his wife and little boy from his breast pocket and gave them each one last kiss. Tears formed in his eyes as he put the pistol into his mouth. It tasted of gun oil and metal. His infected limbs shook more forcefully. He had to bite down on the barrel to keep it in his mouth. Willing his finger muscles to contract, he left this world. The bang reverberated in the tiled bathroom.

*****

In the West Wing of the White House, Mike and his team slowly made their way down the marble spiral staircase. He and his men located the dark wooden door to the White House Situation room. Aside from Mr. Jones and his intern there had been no other infected in the West Wing. The bloody handprints and blood trail in the upstairs hall outside of the Oval Office were the only indication things may have gone sideways on the President and his protection detail. Mike had a sinking feeling there would be no one left alive to tell that story.

The men formed up in front of the wood-paneled titanium blast door. Mike rapped on it with a gloved hand. A series of bumps and bangs answered him back.

In his ear he heard a new report from the other team.

"This is Lowrider, we are enroute to the West Wing. My team is at half strength," Sergeant First Class Lopez said.

"Copy that Lowrider, Cowboy out."

130

Mike got the attention of Warrant Officer Clark and warned him to be ready to receive the three remaining team members, lest they have another friendly fire incident.

Clark nodded in recognition.

During the mission briefing hours ago, Speaker of the House Valerie Clay provided the last known entry code for the situation room. She was the only known surviving member of the U.S. government still communicating with the Joint Chiefs of Staff. Barring the retrieval of a living breathing POTUS or VPOTUS she was the next in order of succession.

Mike touched the keypad and entered the digits he had memorized. The green light on the keypad blinked momentarily before the door slid into the wall, revealing the interior of the situation room and the carnage inside. The smell was noxious and Mike had all he could do to keep his gag reflex in check.

President Odero's hubris kept him from accepting his protective detail's recommendation that he be moved to a safer location. The men and women staffers pleaded with him and the First Lady to allow them to be moved to Iron Mountain as protocol dictated. Instead he recalled all of his cabinet and the Joint Chiefs of Staff back to the White House just hours after declaring martial law. Only a handful of the cabinet members had made it back and none of the Joint Chiefs of Staff returned to 1600 Pennsylvania Avenue. Of the staffers that did return, President Odero's National Security Advisor Daniel Guzman was already infected, thus dooming everyone in the White House.

The source of the banging came forward, a Secret Service Agent, most of his face hanging in strips over the collar of his blood-caked white cotton oxford shirt. His empty leather shoulder holster bounced with his lurching steps, the flesh colored earpiece dangling where his ear used to be swishing to and fro like a bloody pendulum. Jaundiced eyes stared at the soldiers entering the inner sanctum. Somewhere in the recesses of its hippocampus the thing remembered it had something to protect. Mike became its target.

With the precision honed from hours of practicing live fire shooting, the team swept the medium-sized room, each instinctively taking the proper firing zone.

Mike punched out the Secret Service zombie's right eye with a three round burst, crouched low, and crab walked to the right around the massive table flanked by enormous darkened LCD panel televisions.

Seconds elapsed and the rest of the room was cleared of undead. There were six in total: three more agents, the Vice President and his younger trophy wife, last place in death for sure. Mike sensed the movement beyond the next open door before making contact. It was the President. He was now undead. There were defensive bite wounds on his hands and his pants legs were tattered and torn exposing his monogrammed boxer shorts. Handcuffed to his right arm was an aluminum attaché case.

"Calvin, you rolling digital?" Mike bellowed.

"Affirmative sir."

"Tighten on the face then."

"Copy that."

The image that the camera digitally captured didn't resemble the president. His cheeks were sunken; his usual commanding steely stare was replaced by dead, glazed over eyes peering from a waxy alabaster mask.

"Odero is beyond recovery, preparing to terminate POTUS."

Captain Mike Desantos had the President in his sights and thought, *This shouldn't be happening.* His MP7 silently spit lead and the zombie that used to be the most powerful man in the free world crumpled to the thick carpet spilling blood and brain matter from his bullet-riddled skull.

Mike drew his Hard Steel Tanto blade and put his combat boot on the dead President's upturned hand. With three rapid sawing motions of his knife he removed the appendage. The blood slickened handcuff slid from the stump easily. For the first time since the helos dropped the men at the White House, Mike hailed Fort Bragg so they could inform the former Speaker of the House Valerie Clay she was the new POTUS.

"This is Zulu-One, we have recovered the fumble. How copy?"

"Copy that, RTB (return to base) with the football. Reaper-One and Two are refueling, exfil in ten mikes."

"Roger that. Zulu-One."

Two miles away the helicopters that had inserted the team loitered after their last aerial refueling. Arrangements were made to top off their tanks before rendezvousing with the Delta Teams at the White House for the exfil.

Lastly, out of curiosity, Captain Desantos took the expensive white gold Breitling chronograph from the dead President's other wrist. He turned it over and read the engraved inscription, *"For your unending service and dedication-Welcome into the Guild-The Marzenberg Group."*

The watch went into his pocket but the disbelief at the words he had just read wouldn't go away.

Chapter 30
Day 3 - Outskirts of Nampa, Idaho

Leo pulled first watch. His eyes played tricks on him a time or two but he didn't wake anyone or shoot at shadows.

Sheila rapped on the driver's side window causing Leo to literally jump out of his seat an inch or two. Leo smiled when he realized who it was. Shyly, he asked Sheila what she was still doing up.

"I couldn't sleep. Every time I close my eyes I see her face, and I hear her voice constantly. Am I going crazy?" the pretty blonde asked.

"It sucks. Those walking dead motherfuckers suck. Life sucks without my little brother... So to answer your question, no, you are far from crazy. I ain't crazy either. We are just so used to them always being with us," Leo said, looking toward Sheila in the dark.

"I miss her so much!" Sheila started to sob silently, her body wracked with grief. Leo innocently rubbed her shoulder for a few minutes until she composed herself. Sensing that she could use some support he asked, "I was wondering, can I ride with you tomorrow? We can keep each other company."

"Yes... yes you can. Maybe we can distract each other from thinking about... "

They sat in silence with their own thoughts until Cade materialized from the inky darkness ready to take over guard duty. Leo's first impression was that Cade looked like a robot because of the NV goggles on his face.

Leo fell asleep under a sleeping bag on the third bench seat. Sheila slept stretched across the second row while Cade kept watch.

Cade could see his breath when he exhaled; the temperature had dropped off considerably after the sun made its exit. Even though his hands were growing numb from the cold, he kept the window open so he could rely on his sense of smell to warn him of any approaching undead. While keeping one eye on the surroundings he checked his phone for messages. He had no cell service and there were no new messages so he powered it off and turned on the stereo. With the volume turned down very low Cade checked all of the AM and FM stations for news, but all he heard was white noise. There was an hour of watch left for him but he knew the luxury of sleeping afterward was out of the question. During Ranger training and the Special Forces qualifying course he had gone days with little or no sleep. He would do that now because he knew their lives depended on him. Cade also felt a huge responsibility for Leo, especially after what had happened to Ike.

With nothing to do but stare into the dark and listen to the steady rhythmic breathing coming from the back seat, he reflected on the day gone by. It was eerie how deserted the freeways had been. Since leaving Portland they seemed to be the only denizens of the road. Cade guessed that they had found themselves caught between two roadblocks on the interstate. *The government was taking this quarantine thing dead seriously.*

*****

In the distance the pinpoints of light gave them away before the big engines announced their approach. A very raucous group of Harleys passed by at around 3:30 am as Rawley's watch was about to start; they came back a short while later and probed the parking lot with their headlights. They stayed near the rest stop entrance for two or three minutes, motors idling and beating out a deep throated cadence. Cade and Rawley counted four headlights.

"What do you make of that?" Rawley said when the bikers turned and roared off into the Idaho night, red taillights diminishing in the distance.

"They're bandits and they're sizing us up. We've got enough vehicles here that they probably decided to get reinforcements."

135

"Do you gather they're the same murderers Duncan mentioned?"

"Dollars to doughnuts, one and the same," Cade said bleakly.

*****

Everyone awoke at dawn; as soon as the sun arose so did the temperature. It was going to be a hot day in the high desert.

Cade filled the group in on the evening incursion and reminded everyone to stay frosty and be aware of their surroundings. He finished by telling the drivers that in case of an attack or ambush, "Accelerate through the kill zone and regroup. Whatever you do, do not stop!" He spoke slowly and was careful to add extra emphasis on the *do not stop* part.

Breakfast consisted of MREs and bottled water. Weapons were loaded, gas tanks were filled and then the five dusty vehicles exited the rest stop single file.

"This is Rawley, come in."

Cade found it amusing how unnatural Rawley sounded when he talked on the Motorola, considering he used to make a living singing and playing the guitar.

"Copy that," he replied.

A little static came from the speaker. "How about I take the lead for a while?" Rawley asked.

"Copy that," Cade replied again.

Rawley's white Bronco overtook the Sequoia and held a steady forty-five miles an hour while dodging single stalls and slowing considerably for multiple vehicle choke points. On a couple of occasions he put the bull bar on the Bronco to use and handily pushed the stalled cars off of the road.

They were making good time and nearing Nampa, Idaho when they needed to stop to siphon fuel. A group of undead thrashed about in a Chevy Suburban as Rawley nervously emptied its large gas tank of unleaded. He was pretty sure they couldn't unlock the doors, but stranger shit had happened. With one eye on the undead and one eye on the gas can he finally finished his unnerving task. Not wanting to waste ammo he left them to bake in the sun on their eternal road trip.

Leo had taken to riding with Shelly and she also welcomed his company and felt more secure with another person in the car.

Their conversation settled on how things had been growing up with a close sibling and how they had enjoyed the camaraderie, but abhorred the rivalries. Shelly changed the subject and tried to imagine the future without Sheila. Not wanting to think about what was in store for him, Leo clammed up.

*****

Harry's Camaro started running rough soon after they left the rest stop. It was overheating and wouldn't hold water. They inspected under the hood and found a burst hose. Not wanting to attempt a roadside repair, Harry reluctantly decided to leave it on the shoulder. He put his meager belongings into Duncan's truck, got in and rode shotgun. He took one last glance at his fully restored pride and joy and then focused on the road ahead. Being a quiet sensitive kind of guy he was having a hard time coping with the new reality, as well as the loss of his one true accomplishment. He and his wife had lovingly restored that car. Harry was in a real funk that stemmed from the fact he wasn't around to help his wife when the dead started walking. Losing the Camaro was the last straw.

Sensing his sadness Duncan said, "You can get yourself any one of those 2010 models when we find a Chevy lot. And I'm pretty sure that some dead guy walking around out there isn't going to need his classic Camaro… either way I'm sure you'll find a replacement."

"Screw the car. I want to find my wife." Tears were forming in Harry's eyes. "She never came home from the mall the first day of the outbreak. I tried calling the police, the hospitals and her family out of town. Poof! She just vanished."

"Do you have any other family nearby?"

Harry dried his eyes with his sleeve. "No, none whatsoever. My wife has a brother and sister up in Olympia, Washington, but nobody answered their phone when I called. My wife Margaret had been gone less than a day when I tried to report her as missing. They told me that it had to be more than twenty-four hours since there was any contact before they would take a report. I waited and tried to make the report… by then it was too late, the police were not answering anyone's calls. I suspect that they were combating the violence that was breaking out all over the city. Anyway… I couldn't handle the stress. I just started driving."

"I'm sorry man, I had no idea," Duncan commiserated with a pained look on his face. He was clearly embarrassed that he brought up replacing it at all. Being a lifelong bachelor and never really getting along with the fairer sex, Duncan didn't have much to say concerning Harry's wife's disappearance. Besides, he thought, *Women are always leaving me and not coming back.*

"It's OK. I plan on going back and looking for her when the quarantine is lifted and Portland is back to normal. I just followed you people because it was the path of least resistance."

"If there is any way I can help, let me know."

"Thanks Duncan. If I ever do get over losing that Camaro, how about you do the negotiating when we find a car lot? I hate car salesmen anyhow… especially undead ones."

Given the absurdity of their situation, the men laughed at the thought.

They drove on in silence, each man wrestling with his own thoughts.

"Why didn't I think of this earlier?" Duncan asked himself, breaking the quiet and startling Harry. Duncan reached over and punched open the glove box. Inside was a shiny new Citizens Band radio. Duncan answered his own question. "I guess out of sight is as good as out of mind. I never have used this toy anyways."

He turned on the CB radio and asked Harry to scan the channels while he focused on driving. Harry seemed pleased to finally have something to keep him busy.

"Did you catch that?" Harry asked excitedly.

The transmission was faint. On channel fourteen they listened to two men talking about five vehicles on the highway. A light bulb went off in Harry's head. "I'm beginning to think those fellas are talking about our little convoy."

Duncan honked his horn and flashed his lights to alert the others.

The four vehicles crowded close as they slowed and stopped in the middle of the road.

"They're stopping," a man's voice said over the CB.

"Keep an eye on them. Tell me when they move again."

"Roger that. Hey man, they've got a blonde with them."

Harry arched his eyebrows and knowingly looked at Duncan.

"There's the proof. They *are* talking about us. We had better be careful; it doesn't sound like they are watching us for fun."

Cade leaned in the open driver's side window. Harry told him his suspicions and repeated verbatim the conversation they had intercepted.

They listened to the CB for a few minutes.

Cade keyed the two-way and hailed Rawley to fill him in. "No offense but I'm going to take point again."

"No problem, want me to bring up the rear?"

"Yeah, but be extra vigilant and watch your six, we don't know where they're watching us from. I want to give your radio to Harry so he can keep me informed of what they're saying on the CB," Cade said into his Motorola.

Cade walked down the line of vehicles to the Bronco and retrieved the radio from Rawley. *Note to self, we need to find a couple more radios and fresh batteries for the ones we have before they go dead.*

Harry was going to have his hands full, literally, CB in one hand, two-way radio in the other. Once they were on the move again the same voice on channel fourteen continued reporting their actions. If Harry's hunch was right, these people watching them were the same group that had probed them the night before. Harry started to worry.

They drove through open range, interspersed with small stands of trees. They didn't plan on stopping again until the flatland turned hilly and the trees were abundant enough to provide them adequate cover.

Cade's SUV led, followed by the red VW Cabriolet containing Leo and Sheila. Rawley was in the "O.J." Bronco, and Duncan and Harry brought up the rear in the lifted 4x4.

"We're still being watched," Harry reported to Cade on the Motorola.

Cade planned to continue driving until it appeared they were no longer under surveillance, then double back on foot and go on a solo recon of the surrounding hills to find their secret admirers.

The flat open area they had driven through for the last ten miles was finally giving way and they entered a pine tree-lined highway.

Cade registered the out-of-place mound of dirt a second too late. The Sequoia absorbed a fraction of the blast, just enough to move the big rig a little. In the mirror he saw the little red VW disappear in the violent explosion, recipient of the bulk of the energy and shrapnel.

Cade remembered all too well the distinctive sound of automatic weapons fire and bullets impacting sheet metal. These first sounds of an ambush were engraved in his memory from his time spent in the sandbox.

"Do not stop!" he screamed into the hand-held Motorola. The first order of business was to get out of the kill zone.

The remaining two vehicles rolled through the blast area and took sporadic fire; they had to swerve to avoid the carcass of the little convertible. As he passed by, Rawley was high enough off of the ground to see into the smoking VW. Under the shredded remains of the soft-top, Sheila and Leo were still moving. Rawley started to slow his Bronco while anxiously glancing in the rear view mirror, but thought better of it. A side quarter window on his passenger side exploded. Gunfire continued pouring from the woods.

The Sequoia and the Dodge were safely out of the kill zone but the white Bronco lagged behind. Cade abruptly braked and stopped in the middle of the road. Duncan nearly collided with him but managed to squeeze the big 4x4 by on the right and perform a U-turn to form up next to the Sequoia. They had stopped several hundred yards from where the attack had taken place.

Back at the ambush site undead emerged from the woods, shambling towards the wreck.

Rawley watched helplessly in his rearview mirror as the ghouls arrived at the stationary car and began tearing apart the boy and the young lady he secretly had taken a liking to. Making an emotional snap decision, he applied the brakes. The Bronco's tires chirped, belching blue smoke. He made the Bronco do a one-eighty, stopped in place momentarily, and then raced back to the horrific scene. While driving one-handed, he depressed the thumb switch for the laser on the SKS assault rifle and flicked the safety off. Next he pushed a button on the dash that started the motorized sunroof opening. Screeching to a halt, he put the Bronco in park and stood up in the sunroof shouldering his rifle. The zombie he targeted had no idea there was a red dot painting its gray forehead; the only thing it knew was that it needed to eat. A 7.62 bullet stopped the need.

Leo and Shelly had initially suffered dreadful mortal wounds from the blast. The undead sped up the process as they stripped the pair of their flesh from the waist up. Rawley watched as they both started to reanimate and were now fighting to escape their seatbelts. Saying a heartfelt "Sorry" under his breath, Rawley shot Leo through the temple, ceasing his struggles. He painted the laser beam on what used to be Sheila, his finger tightening on the trigger. His head was blown apart by a supersonic .50 caliber bullet before the command from his brain could make his finger pull the trigger.

*****

Randall Trask was enraged that his spotter had detonated the device two seconds too late, not to mention the fact that the other penetrator IED failed totally. His incompetence ensured some of them would escape. *Dumb fuck was probably stoned.*

The moment Trask saw the pink vapor through the scope and watched the man's headless torso slump over the windshield, the former-Marine scout sniper knew he had another confirmed kill. He caressed the hog's tooth hanging from his neck while he waited for "dumb fuck" to spot another target for him.

"I think the other two trucks got away," the spotter said, stammering nervously.

"Keep glassing idiot."

The skinny spotter watched the baited zombies. They were clumsily trying to get at the bottom half of the man stuck in the white SUV. Since the windows were only half way open, it was going to take them awhile to eat the cooling corpse.

*****

Earlier that day as the rising sun washed the Idaho foothills with golden light, the shooter and his spotter watched the men prepare the ambush site on the road below. Jerrod dug the holes for the two devices; they were roughly two hundred feet apart. When the digging was finished the zombie bait was strung up. The two men had survived the previous day's ambush. Now they both wished that they hadn't. It took an hour for them to bleed to death; the two in the sniper hide watched the men suffer terribly as the ghouls ate them from the feet up. Not only did it provide morbid entertainment, it also guaranteed there would be undead milling around the kill zone.

*****

Cade observed the Bronco slew around, stop, and accelerate in the other direction through the haze from the smoking tires. He watched it all unfold in slow motion knowing that Rawley was out of control and putting his life in danger.

The moment Rawley's head disintegrated, Cade knew that his new friend was dead. He had been on the giving end of a Barrett .50 caliber sniper rifle and had seen firsthand, magnified thirty times, the damage it could inflict. Shaking his head bitterly, he knew there was nothing he could have done to change the outcome.

Chapter 31
Day 3 - 15 miles from Boise, Idaho

As soon as the bomb went off, Jerrod opened the gate on the horse trailer and watched as the rest of the zombies surged towards the road. So far without fail every caravan except for this one had stopped immediately to help their traveling companions. The walkers proved to be the perfect way to find out if they were armed, or how much fight they had in them.

Jerrod was giddy with excitement as he climbed down from his tree stand. This was the sixth time they had staged an ambush on this highway, never in the same place though and each time the outcome had been different. Sometimes there were women survivors. That was what Jerrod hoped for this morning. It reminded him of Christmas because Randall Trask, his mentor and former employer, let him keep some of the spoils gained from their exploits. That's also how Jerrod got his very first lay and the AR-15 he now carried. He was hooked after his first ambush. As grateful to Randall that he was, it would only be a matter of time before the government would regroup and start to restore order. After the infection was sorted out and all of the walking dead were dispatched they would come calling. This, Jerrod was certain of.

Before the outbreak he had worked for Mr. Trask at his gun store. Eventually he wanted to join the Navy SEALs and become a sniper. Now his only goal was to take some ill-begotten supplies and hopefully a girl back to his dad's compound up North. There was no way Jerrod was going to stick around. When the United States military came looking for their missing soldiers, he would be long gone.

From a safe distance he watched the zombies attack the two people in the small red car. The other ghouls were a sight to see as they tried to get to the remains of the driver in the Bronco. Smart ass racist that he was, Jerrod said out loud, "Donner, party of five. Will we be having white meat or dark?" He laughed like a maniac at his own joke while the black kid and white girl were dying. Jerrod's comrades climbed down from their tree stands and cautiously edged towards the highway.

*****

Trask had appointed Jerrod the official zombie wrangler, even going so far as to try to convince him it was a prestigious posting. This was a dangerous job but Jerrod was used to the dog catcher's pole. On the user's end there was another loop of wire that had to be pulled to tighten the noose. It was very effective and it kept the undead out of biting range. The other men helped prod the infected in the direction of their makeshift pen. If the world ever returned to something that resembled normal, at least Jerrod had found his calling. He figured he would make a hell of an animal control officer.

While Jerrod hurriedly locked the horse trailer, the other men pulled Rawley's headless body from the Bronco and started a thorough search. One of the attackers let out a wild rebel yell and held up the SKS carbine, showing off his prize to the others and then rattling off twenty rounds into Rawley's headless corpse.

Hearing the distant gunfire, Cade grabbed his M4 and sought cover off of the road. Duncan drove his truck into a copse of trees. He and Harry joined Cade inside of the tree line. There, the three discussed their next move.

Cade would go it alone. He could move faster and quieter that way. First he wanted to get info on the size of force they were dealing with. If the opportunity presented itself he would kill as many as of them as possible. The ruthless way these fuckers operated had turned this into a personal vendetta for him.

Harry and Duncan would stay behind with the vehicles and keep in contact with Cade on the hour. It was decided that if he failed to make radio contact two times in a row, they would leave the keys to the Sequoia on a predetermined tree branch nearby and then continue on in Duncan's truck.

Cade extracted the long canvas bag from the back of the Sequoia; he removed his ballistic vest and knee pads, and then swapped his Blazers cap for the flat black, low profile, tactical Kevlar helmet. Cade randomly applied camouflage paint to his face and neck. Lastly he extracted his Remington Modular Sniper Rifle from the bag. The gun was chambered in .338 Lapua Magnum and had a magazine that held ten rounds. It was very easy to carry with the stock folded and the suppressor removed. Cade slung the weapon over his shoulder and picked up his trusty M4.

"Stay frosty," was all he said before he slipped into the thicket of trees bordering the road and stealthily padded in the direction they had come from.

*****

Hunkered down, he watched from cover as the four attackers looted the food, weapons and anything of value from the Bronco.

The VW was still burning with the bodies of Leo and Sheila inside. Their blackened corpses were frozen in death and still appeared to be wrestling with the now molten seatbelts.

The Bronco leaned on two flat tires, both on the passenger side. After dragging Rawley's headless body off of the road, one of the men started the Bronco and used it to push the blackened hulk of steel, which used to resemble a car, off of the asphalt. He then drove the useless SUV into the trees and abandoned it there.

It appeared the attackers were getting ready to bug out. Like a ghost, Cade silently moved through the trees, his head constantly scanning, the lethal carbine held at low ready.

*****

Harry stayed concealed, cradling the Mossberg and trying to remain alert. Duncan was on the other side of the median armed with his shotgun. They would be waiting for Cade to make contact, every hour on the hour, either by voice or with two microphone clicks if he couldn't respond verbally.

Chapter 32
Day 2 - Lumberton, North Carolina

The truck lurched a few times well before the engine began coughing and sputtering. The fuel gauge read only a tick above empty. Carl pointed the truck towards the new car lot two blocks away. They made it only one.

With a deadpan look plastered on his face Carl said, "We're going to have to get that gas gauge replaced. Never know when we'll run out of gas in a bad neighborhood."

Without hesitating, Brook and Carl each grabbed one of the new shotguns. Raven was able to carry the small bag of food they had taken from the vending machines. Reluctantly Brook left her late father's Ithaca in the stalled truck; she shuddered at the thought of how she had saved their lives with it back in Myrtle Beach.

Weapons in hand, they emerged from the cab of the utility truck. Raven jumped down and hefted the bag over her shoulder, its weight apparent as she hobbled like a little old lady.

There were five walkers between them and their objective. Carl pointed at the blue oval sign a block ahead; it read "Romero's Lumberton Ford."

"That's where we are going. We need to be as quiet as possible. Remember, stealth is our friend."

The closest walker was a petite elderly woman; she walked hunched over and resembled Yoda from Star Wars. Her skin had a greenish hue and she had the same sparse, wispy white hair. Using the shotgun as a club, Carl bashed her in the head and then stomped it for good measure after she fell. The stuff that came out was black and viscous and stayed on his shoes.

The next undead obstacle looked like a more formidable foe. The large young male wore a gothic get up: flared black jeans three sizes too big and a ripped and faded Marilyn Manson tee shirt. His multiple facial piercings suffered from the decomposition. Some had popped out and the ones that remained oozed yellowish-green pus. Goth ghoul was a bit faster than the little old lady. Brook started name calling to get his attention. He was faster than she had fathomed and somehow managed to wrap one of his cold clammy arms around her neck. Before he could take a bite Carl clubbed him from behind. He fell in a heap at their feet. Gray brain matter soiled the shotgun's stock. "I hate when that happens," Carl said as he wiped the brains off on Marilyn Manson's silkscreened face.

"I owe you one big brother. I would have shot him, but I didn't want to accidentally hit you or Raven."

"No worries, Sis. I'm actually proud of you. You didn't scream like a girl."

"I tried. Nothing would come out." She winked at him.

Raven was still rooted to the spot from where she had witnessed the whole melee.

Brook waved her hand in front of her shocked daughter's face and brought her back to the living. She pulled her along by the arm, helping the trio pick up their pace. Carl did a stutter step feint to get them around the third shambling ghoul and onto the car lot. The pursuing walkers continued their ghostly moans. A very noisy low flying Apache helicopter momentarily drew their attention. It was the distraction the pursued needed as they wove their way between the rows of gleaming cars and trucks. Carl and Brook pulled on door handles as they passed by each of the new vehicles. All were locked up tight.

The moaning from the undead in pursuit attracted more walkers from the Walgreens across the street, causing a stinking exodus of corpses moving towards the dealership.

"Let's get inside the showroom. Keep your eyes open for keys or preferably a lock box full of them," Carl said as he reached the glass double doors and yanked on the handles with both hands. To his amazement they were unlocked and swung freely outward.

"Let go and let God," Carl said, reciting one of his favorite A.A. sayings. "Wow, I haven't even thought about a drink yet, even with the end of the world looming."

Pushing Raven through the open doors while staying close on his heels, Brook said to her brother, "This isn't the time to be twelve-stepping. If we don't get some wheels soon, *I am going to need a drink.*"

"Hurry up! They're getting closer... and there are more coming from across the street!" Raven's voice was much higher pitched than normal, the overwhelming stress evident in it.

After everyone was inside, Carl felt along the door's edge, searching for the locking mechanism. To his dismay he found that there was no way to lock the doors without a special key. He groaned when he read the sign that stated, "These doors should always remain unlocked during normal business hours."

"I can't *find* the fucking lock!" Carl blurted out, the exasperation showing on his sweat-soaked face.

The undead were closing in. Two had arrived at the still unlocked doors. Brook poked her shotgun through the open crack and discharged it pointblank in the nearest ghoul's face. It dropped to its knees and fell motionless, blocking the doors. Carl removed his belt and quickly wound it between the push-bars of each door. As a makeshift lock it might hold for a few minutes, scarcely enough time to search the expansive showroom and offices for the keys to a getaway vehicle. A lone walker impacted the security glass with a loud bang, discharge from its festering face painting a trail of gore everywhere it touched. The undead marched onto the lot, wending their way around the new Fords towards the treats in the indoor showroom.

"I'll hold the doors while you look for keys," Carl said as he observed the zombies slam dance with the doors.

"I tried the sales manager's office... but the door is locked!"

"Where the hell is Raven?" Carl asked Brook, looking around frantically.

A loud earsplitting roar followed by a deep toned, idling engine momentarily deafened them in the enclosed showroom.

Carl and Brook nearly pissed their pants as they both visibly started.

"Found the keys!" Raven said, beaming from the driver's seat of the bright orange Ford Raptor 4x4 pickup. "The keys were in it already. I hoped it would start." With a mischievous grin she added, "I'm driving, right...?"

"Move over, squirt," Carl said to the little heroine.

Brook threw herself into the passenger seat with her daughter wedged in the middle.

How did I not see this big orange monstrosity? Carl thought, shaking his head back and forth. He put the transmission in drive and marveled at the power and torque as he launched the truck at the large glass doors it was facing.

"Brace yourselves."

Like an orange missile, the race bred off-road truck shattered the glass with a thunderous crash. They all held on as the truck easily mowed down the walkers in its path. Carl let out an adrenaline induced scream as he deftly maneuvered the Raptor through the maze of vehicles and walking dead clogging the lot. After making short work of a dozen undead, the Raptor leapt off of the curb nearly sideswiping a row of brand new Ford F-150 trucks. *Good going Dale Jr., we're trying to survive a pandemic and I nearly kill us all.*

Carl took his eyes off of the road long enough to glance at the gas gauge to find that the tank was full. A bit of relief washed over him because he knew this should be enough to deliver them to the military base without the need to stop again. They headed for Fayetteville, thirty miles to the northeast. Brook made the observation first, that what little traffic there was, streamed from the other direction.

"Honey, that was a good thing you did back there, I am real proud of you. However *do not* leave my sight from this moment forward!"

"I'll second that, little bird. When I couldn't find you, I panicked thinking the worst," Carl said, patting her softly on the head without removing his eyes from the road.

On the other side of the freeway many of the vehicles heading their way were military, mainly Humvee and deuce and a half troop transports. It appeared the people were finally leaving the big cities, against the President's recommendation.

The big special purpose off-road production truck was race ready and proved it more than once. It rolled on massive wheels and tires and was sprung with eleven inches of travel. They effortlessly skirted around wrecks, humans trying to flag them down and the numerous walking dead they came across. Carl made a sport of driving over any of the bastards that got in his way; he wasn't worried about the thirty-five inch off-road tires becoming punctured.

They passed through the cities of Nakina, Bladenboro and Tar Heel. All had a huge undead population and seemed to be void of living humans.

On the outskirts of the farming community Tar Heel, Brook had to once again put the blinders on her daughter. The undead had gotten into an enclosure filled with a substantial herd of cows. While the bovines were still alive, the blood soaked monsters burrowed into their bellies to get at their entrails. The mournful sound of the dying cows caused the hair on Brook's arms to stand on end.

Their greatest obstacle, Fayetteville, North Carolina, loomed twenty-four miles ahead and was undoubtedly teeming with infected. The traffic was almost at a standstill coming towards them and many more undead attacks were happening on the other side of the median among the slowed line of vehicles. In order to escape the chaos, cars and SUVs started to navigate across the grass separating the eastbound and westbound lanes.

"Are we going to go through Fayetteville proper?" Brook asked.

"What do you think, sis?"

Before Brook could answer, an oncoming Suburban engaged them in a game of chicken. At the last moment Carl wrenched the steering wheel to the right, grass and mud erupting in a geyser from the Raptor's knobby tires as they were forced onto the shoulder. After the near miss, Brook took a minute to calm down enough to answer Carl's question.

"I think it would be safer if we were to double back and go around the city. The traffic is only going to get worse and the amount of undead seems to be increasing."

Carl was very cautious after the near miss. He slowed the Raptor to a crawl, left the paved road and followed the Suburban in the direction they had just come from.

A dull throb in his lower lumbar caused Carl to squirm in his seat; the deep scratch marks on his back started to itch and seep blood. Ignoring the discomfort and the possibility the ghoul may have signed his death warrant, Carl focused on avoiding the sporadic oncoming traffic.

Chapter 33
Day 3 - Outskirts of Boise, Idaho

Cade smelled the undead long before he saw them. They were locked up in a horse trailer secreted inside of the tree line. He was very careful to give a wide enough berth so they wouldn't start their god-awful moaning and give him away.

He had been stalking the four men for twenty minutes and watched them as they reached the top of the hill, lingering longer than necessary. This slip up confirmed that they had little or no military training. Any soldier would know how to use the "military crest" of a hill to mask their movement and limit silhouetting themselves.

He wondered where these amateurs had stolen their desert ACUs. Using the binoculars he determined they were wearing authentic U.S. uniforms with insignia, name and rank. It appeared they were AWOL Idaho National Guardsmen. His sixth sense was really telling him something different. These definitely were not United States trained soldiers. He was stalking imposters.

The four men crossed the westbound lanes and headed straight for the foothills in the distance. They moved slowly because they were loaded down with all they had looted from the attack.

Cade was going to follow the murderous brigands to their staging grounds and lay dog and observe until he had a firm grasp of how many he would be killing.

The terrain was perfect for tracking. It was high desert and dusty and there were lots of small to medium juniper and other hardy scrub brush to conceal a pursuer. Not only were the men oblivious to noise discipline, they were leaving MRE food wrappers in their wake as they ascended the hill.

The camp was on a large piece of land a short hike from the interstate. On one end of the grassy plot was a giant mound of gravel. Parked nearby were three Idaho Department of Transportation sanding trucks. On the other end of the land was a broad expanse of grass where the biker horde had set up camp. Four fifth-wheel trailers were arranged in a semicircle on the back side of a small hill. One of the pickups was detached from its trailer; the other three were still connected.

To his amazement he noticed two military Humvees, painted in desert camouflage, partially hidden behind the trailers. One of the Hummers was a gun truck with a Dillon minigun mounted in the bed. Cade and his team had used similar ones in the sandbox. The vehicles were positioned for a quick getaway where they couldn't be seen from the interstate.

There were numerous brightly colored tents of all different shapes and sizes dotting the clearing. The grass was trampled everywhere he looked. Judging by the many old campfire pits and the trash strewn about, he knew there would be scores of people returning to spend the night.

Suddenly a large man with a flowing black beard walked out of the brush to the left of the circled trailers. He wore the same desert fatigues as the men Cade had tracked; a floppy boonie hat was pulled down low over his eyes. His head was constantly moving, scanning his surroundings. Cade could tell at once that this man was nothing like the others; he walked with confidence and purpose, he moved like an operator. Cade recognized the Barrett M-82 sniper rifle the man carried by its distinct outline and large wedge shaped muzzle brake. It was fitted with a high powered scope and could deliver a hefty .50 caliber bullet out to 5,900 feet. Cade had a feeling he was looking at the man who had killed Rawley.

A second man emerged from the brush. He was in civilian clothes and didn't seem as confident as the first man. He carried a very large spotting scope and slung over his shoulder was an AR-15.

The sniper went inside the unhooked trailer and slammed the door behind him. In response to the loud noise, a man in fatigues poked his head out of another trailer and emerged, appearing to guard the camp. Shortly thereafter the other three men that Cade had tracked to the camp filed out of the same trailer, beer bottles in hand.

The bearded man reemerged into the clearing and although they were out of Cade's earshot, it looked like he was calling the men over for a group meeting. He was definitely in charge. Cade could tell by the body language of the other men.

The youngest of the group produced a bag with the food and supplies pillaged from the ambush; the big man poured it out on the ground and divided the contents. The kid also handed over the SKS assault rifle and after a cursory inspection the bearded leader handed it back to him.

Cade keyed the Motorola and hailed Harry. Holding the radio so that both he and Duncan could hear, he answered, "This is Harry. Duncan is listening in."

"I'm laying dog and watching a large camp with at least twenty tents but so far I've only seen six personnel, all armed. I'm a mile and a half northwest of your position. It looks like most of the people that were here are out and about, so stay alert. Cade out."

"OK, roger that," Harry replied.

Cade watched the camp through his binoculars. The five men arranged folding camp chairs and sat in a semicircle drinking long neck Buds, which they replenished from a big silver cooler.

For thirty minutes they drank and carried on a very animated conversation. He took note; the youngest amongst them was nursing his beer. Judging by the amount of empties, the other men were on at least beer number three.

The door to one of the trailers flew open with a bang. The bearded sniper emerged with a petite woman in tow. She was naked and appeared bruised and battered; her long red hair was wrapped around his ham sized fist. She looked mentally broken, her eyes locked on the ground.

Cade put down the binoculars and retrieved his sniper rifle; through the scope he watched as another man violently took hold of the woman's wrist and walked her away from the camp towards the woods. Cade recognized him as the same man that had been spotting for the sniper. *This mutt needs to die.* He kept the crosshairs trained on the skinny man's neck. If he took the shot while they were moving then it would unnecessarily put the redheaded woman in danger, plus he didn't want to alert the bad guys to his presence just yet.

The two were nearly at the tree line. A metallic whirring sound carried on the light breeze from the clearing below; Cade recognized it for what it was the instant he heard it. He still had the man and woman scoped and he watched them disappear in an explosion of flesh, organs, bone and pink-misted blood. The bearded leader had covertly made his way to the Humvee and was now manning the 7.62 mm Dillon minigun mounted to the gun truck. He released a 300 round burst, leaving the pile of human remains seeping into the dirt.

Shifting his aim to just below and behind the man's left eye, Cade adjusted for elevation and windage. He relaxed his breathing. *This one's for you, Rawley,* he thought as he gently caressed the trigger. The suppressed rifle coughed once. It was a perfect head shot, and the waste of skin fell atop the minigun, the top half of his head nonexistent, leaving only his bushy black beard and jawbone still attached at the neck.

The four other men fell to the ground, desperately looking in all directions for the shooter. Cade smirked as the fat man hid behind his green canvas camp chair. *Peek-a-boo asshole, this one's for Leo.* The .338 Lapua round went through the makeshift fabric shield and shattered the man's sternum before lodging in his heart, killing him instantly.

Shocked and in total disbelief, Jerrod slowly commando crawled under the nearest trailer. He didn't want to be the next victim of the unseen shooter. Shaking off the little buzz the beer had given him, he shimmied out from under cover and quickly snared the SKS by the sling and launched himself into the underbrush, then patiently crawled away from the slaughter.

Cade chambered another round and watched the remaining three men low crawl, attempting to take cover near the Humvee's front bumper. Cade saw the terror evident on the man's face magnified through the scope. The bullet impacted above his upper lip and proceeded upward into his nasal cavity. The velocity of the round peeled his face away from the skull, rendering him unrecognizable. The man cowering near him was showered with human detritus. "One shot one kill" is the sniper's motto, and so far

Cade was living up to it. It almost wasn't fair. The grown man was visibly sobbing, his body heaved up and down as he struggled for air. The balding spot on the crown of the man's head was where the cross hairs rested. Cade mouthed the words, "And this one's for you, Sheila," as he sent the man to Hell.

The youngest of the four men that had been drinking beers around the cooler was the only one left. Cade had no idea where he had gone, but he knew he wouldn't stray far.

Ever so slowly he backed down from the slight berm he had set up his over watch behind. The sagebrush concealed him from any eyes below as he patiently disassembled the sniper rifle, first folding the stock and then removing the suppressor. It was a hunch, but he had a strong feeling that the kid would fall back and hide out, waiting for his friends to return.

*****

What have I gotten myself into now? Jerrod thought as he slowly tried to flank the shooter. His best guess was that the sniper must have been on the hill facing the circle of trailers. There was no way the headshot that took out Trask could have come from the trees behind them.

*****

There was a shuffling sound, followed by the sharp snap of a twig. Cade bent to one knee and swept his M4 towards the sound. Slowly scanning his surroundings, he perceived movement at his eleven o'clock. The young man crept into view; he was a rookie and didn't use any of the available cover to his advantage. Suddenly he went to ground and low crawled through some underbrush. *He is pretty brave or just plain stupid trying to out sneak a sniper.* He let the kid get comfortable and then silently approached from behind with the M4 at the ready. Rawley's SKS was in the kid's possession; this was going to have to be handled quietly, up close and personal.

*****

Jerrod was hyperventilating, just like he did when he played paintball with his buddies back at the compound. This was for real and he tried to calm down but he couldn't, he could hear his blood rushing in his head and his heartbeat pounding in his chest. It was like this the first time he had sex a couple of days ago. He didn't want to, but everyone else had raped her already and it happened to be his turn. The other guys heckled and cajoled. It didn't take much though. She looked at him with those dead eyes, silently pleading to get it over with and leave. Jerrod unbuckled his pants and found he was ready. It lasted fifteen seconds, but he stayed in the trailer for another ten minutes lying next to the redheaded woman, not ashamed at what he had done but at how quick it was. The last time, earlier today before the ambush, was better because he lasted a little longer and actually got it in before he ejaculated; she gave him a smart ass smile that made him lose it. He punched and kicked her until somebody came in and pulled him away. He had beaten her badly. *Bitch had it coming, too.* Deep in thought with a dull throbbing in his groin was how he died, the ten inch Gerber carving him ear to ear, severing his carotid artery and slicing through his trachea and vertebrae, nearly severing his head. Cade stabbed the dagger in the dirt, stared deep into the dying man's eyes and watched the life ebb from him. Cade cleaned his knife on the kid's fatigues and repossessed Rawley's prized SKS before descending on the quiet camp.

The Humvees bore markings of the Oregon National Guard and had bullet holes pockmarking the Kevlar bodies. It was evident that the bandits had overtaken a military convoy or checkpoint somewhere and stolen the vehicles, uniforms, weapons and explosives. The latter they had been using to make their roadside bombs. Cade found three pounds of C4 plastic explosives as well as the radio frequency detonators and remotes needed to set off the charges. The Guardsmen may have been engineers sent to drop the bridges on the border and possibly set up a checkpoint. If that were the case, then drastic measures were being undertaken to slow the pathogen's rapid spread.

Wasting no time, he went about setting five half-pound C4 charges. One was affixed to each propane tank on the four travel trailers; he buried the last brick of C4 and placed the cooler over the disturbed soil.

Each C4 block had a radio frequency detonator embedded in the soft putty surface. They all worked on the same frequency and would detonate at the same time. One push of the button on the small plastic remote would unleash hell on anyone in the vicinity. Cade made certain the devices were armed and put the little black box in the cargo pocket of his ACUs.

Cade was in the act of placing the dead bodies around the cooler when he heard the distinctive sound of Harley Davidsons... a lot of them. Luckily for him the road leading to the campsite was potholed enough to slow their approach. He knifed his way through the brush keeping a low profile. Given all of the engine noise, Cade didn't need to worry about stealth. He made it back to his hide before the bad guys arrived. The bikers dismounted and gawked at the three dead men. Cade had hastily arranged them on the folding camp chairs around the booby trapped cooler. In death they appeared to be shooting the breeze over beers.

A large number of the Nomad Jesters were crowded around the seated dead men when Cade remotely detonated the charges. There was an initial ear splitting *WHOOMPH*. Cade burrowed face-first into the fine silt, his head protected by the tactical helmet. The immense heat from the exploding propane tanks warmed his back. Now secondary explosions boomed. The two Humvees were fully engulfed. The ammo onboard started cooking off. The steady pop, pop, pop of various calibers of bullets discharging filled the air. Every trailer down below was now in the process of becoming a molten pool of aluminum. The propane tanks were of the larger variety and added more fuel to the fire. It was no surprise that no pleas for help or screams came from ground zero. Burning bodies and body parts were strewn everywhere. The human toll appeared to be immense. He had no remorse for the biker's "old ladies." Cade considered anyone associated with this crew to be less than human; even though he hadn't seen the big redhead's demise, he was satisfied. Whoever had said "Revenge was a dish best served cold" hadn't seen an inferno like this. Cade watched the flames lick towards the row of fallen motorcycles; they had been knocked down like dominos from the blast. One by one the bikes caught fire. The heat from the flames warmed his face even at this distance. Cade thought about Harry and Duncan; they were probably beside themselves wondering what was happening.

The radio was on the lowest volume setting so he turned it up a notch.

"Come in, come in. Are you there Cade?"

It was Harry's voice.

Click, Click, was Cade's response. He policed up his pack and weapon and then took a different route back to the two men waiting for him.

*****

His leather jacket was starting to catch fire when the man came to. He knew the popping sounds that he was hearing weren't due to enemy gunfire; still he kept his head down as he crawled away from the immolated Humvees lest a stray bullet do what the booby-trapped camp had failed to do. Richard Ganz was blessed that he had to piss when he did. Several of his lieutenants also stopped to provide security. He was a survivor and always would be. Save for a few bruises and a wicked headache he was unscathed. Richard Ganz swore to himself he would track down the son of a bitch that took out his second-in-command and most of his foot soldiers, even if it killed him. The redhead wasted no time; he started barking out orders to his surviving underlings.

Chapter 34
Day 2 - Detour around Fayetteville, North Carolina

Carl was getting used to the basics of driving the race tuned production truck. It was borderline dangerous how fast he could drive the thing while off road and still feel in total control. They had made the decision to take a hundred mile detour around Fayetteville to avoid the majority of the traffic and the growing number of undead.

The route took them west and then north. Route 1 sliced through a rustic town. A green sign at the entrance read *"Aberdeen - founded in 1893. Pop. 3900."* It appeared that nearly all were not of the living, breathing variety. They passed the old train station that was now a tourist site. A static red caboose sat on the grounds. Stranded on the roof of the train car was a blonde boy, his arms waving frantically. He was dressed in shorts and tank top and appeared badly sunburned. Undead were crowding around the wheels of the converted caboose, reaching upward towards him.

Raven noticed the boy first and elbowed her mom, while wildly pointing in his direction.

"Look Mom, look on top of the red train. We need to help him. Uncle Carl, stop…"

"We can't risk all of our lives for a stranger, sweetie," he said looking past Brook at his niece.

Grimacing at the sight of Carl's wrecked face, Brook said, "Put yourself in that boy's shoes Carl…" her voice trailing off, her eyes boring into his.

"Sis... you always did bring home the strays."

"Come on Carl. It's two against one. Turn this beast around."

Raven added, "He really needs our help. Come on Uncle Carl." She could have talked her way into Disneyland with the look she gave him.

Slightly crestfallen, Carl maneuvered the orange Raptor back towards the tourist trap. Dirt, gravel and rocks spewing from the tires pelted the small group of walkers. They didn't flinch or seem affected in the least.

The boy was pacing back and forth from one end of the caboose to the other. It was a large train car that housed a gift shop and snack bar.

"That roof is at least fifteen feet from the ground. The little guy would probably get hurt from the fall or pounced on by those monsters the minute he hit the ground," Carl said.

"Then we need to lure as many of the dead away from the boy that we can and double back and somehow get him to jump into the truck bed," Brook retorted, seeming to want to stay in the middle of the action.

Carl aimed the truck's brush guard at the zombies and turned on the truck's stereo; he scanned the FM stations finding nothing. Next he tried the AM stations, still nothing. Then he punched the CD button hoping that a disc had been left in the changer. After a brief pause, four long drawn out tolls of a church bell spit forth from the ten speaker system, followed by AC/DC's heavy metal song *Hells Bells*. That got the undivided attention of the undead; they nearly broke their necks trying to locate the source of the music.

The railway museum on the far side of the gravel parking lot began to disgorge more of the ghouls; they were attracted to the new meat in the noisy vehicle.

A portly walker, stomach bloated and distended, entered the truck's path and was promptly introduced to the bumper. Like a pudgy bowling ball the zombie bounced and rolled, knocking down three other walkers in the process, finally stopping face down in the dusty gravel. Carl whirled the truck into a complete one eighty, and for good measure, took the opportunity to drive over all of them.

Brook had ahold of the grab handle on the roof as the truck's suspension absorbed the bodies. Raven had nothing to hang onto

161

and bounced around the interior like a rag doll. Brook powered down her window and started hooting and hollering at the walkers, further enticing them to follow.

They hesitated long enough to let some of the undead get tantalizingly close, and then Carl gunned the truck forward a few more feet. It proved to be a smelly game of cat and mouse but it was working. The stink was becoming unbearable with the windows down. Pinching her nose to ward off the stench, Raven joined in on the chorus of catcalls. The orange Ford Raptor acted like a rolling Pied Piper, leading the rotting stinking corpses away from the kid on the roof.

All of the solitary walkers that got in the way were promptly mowed over. Carl charged through a particularly large group of the creatures with the truck, but it proved to be too much and a number of them became wedged underneath.

"Oh no. *Please* shake loose… come on!"

Carl turned the steering wheel hard to the right, throwing the truck into a series of tight donuts. Several dizzying revolutions later the corpses that had been stuck in the undercarriage were expelled. After being reduced to a bunch of skinned carcasses, one stubborn zombie miraculously arose and slowly limped after them, dragging one mangled leg behind it.

The undead had discovered the open door of the caboose and were now cramming themselves inside. This left the outside, for the time being, virtually zombie free. Because of the music and commotion many more walkers streamed from the Railroad Museum, their moans almost drowning out the AC/DC and the Raptor's growling engine. Ignoring the truck, they all headed for the stranded boy.

Brook racked the slide on the shotgun and then gestured by pointing her finger towards the backside of the caboose.

"Go around back. It looked like there were less of those bastards back there."

Carl plowed the truck through a small mob of undead between them and the stranded kid. One of the ghouls cartwheeled up onto the hood of the 4x4. The windshield buckled from the impact, black hair and blood staining the glass. In the rearview mirror Carl saw the ghoul land hard, roll and lay still. Carl threaded the truck through more walkers and pulled alongside of the train car. Brook poked her head out of the window and yelled for the boy to jump.

His terrified face made an appearance over the edge. A moment later he reemerged. With a display of amazing courage, he leaped and cleared the space between the roof and the truck bed. He landed with a clatter, ending up sprawled facedown.

As soon as the boy landed in the truck the walkers changed direction and continued their relentless pursuit.

Too many zombies had accumulated in front of the truck for them to drive forward. The monsters were frantically crawling over each other to get into the vehicle. The ones nearest pounded on the windows with their bony hands. Brook shot a newly turned female zombie in the face and watched her drop, dark blood seeping into the gravel. She chambered another round and with a pull of the trigger dispatched one more stinking corpse. *I think I may have found my calling,* Brook thought as she dramatically blew the smoke from the barrel of her stubby shotgun.

While Brook was dispatching undead, the boy found his footing and peered into the truck's rear window to see who his rescuers were. Carl threw his head around to look out the rear window of the truck. The boy screamed at the sight of the bloody, buckshot- and glass-peppered face staring at him. All he could see were white eyes and teeth. If it weren't for the glass separating the boy from the thing looking at him, he would have jumped out of the truck's bed. Much to the boy's amazement the zombie spoke.

"Stay down and hold on to something," Carl yelled through the glass at the top of his lungs. Wide eyed and openmouthed the boy silently nodded and disappeared from view.

The truck's transmission whined as their speed reached thirty miles per hour in reverse. Carl whipped the wheel around while inadvertently hitting the brakes, resulting in a perfectly executed bootlegger's reverse. It looked like he knew what he was doing.

The boy bounced off of every side of the truck bed before finding a hand hold, muffled exclamations and groans punctuating each impact.

Dodging walkers and wrecked cars they made for the highway. At the interstate they turned left on the final push towards Fort Bragg and hopefully safety.

Carl looked at the gas gauge as the sign urging them to "Return to Aberdeen Soon" flashed by. "Over my dead body," Carl said in response to the request on the sign. Noticing they still had a half of a tank gave him a reason to be somewhat grateful.

Brook reached behind her and slid open the rear window. "My name is Brook. Don't worry, everything is going to be OK. Hold on and keep your head down and we'll pull over as soon as it's safe," she yelled to be heard over the road noise and rushing wind.

Chapter 35
Day 2 - White Sulphur Springs, West Virginia

The four Special Ops helicopters put down on the meticulously manicured lawn that separated the granite and marble architectural marvel from the thirty six-hole golf course. The Greenbrier in West Virginia was built in the fifties and was totally remodeled during Reagan's years in office. Originally a country club, it was now the seat of power for the U.S. government. It held vast underground caverns and stored everything two hundred people would need to survive for three years. An aquifer ran under the property and the air inside was scrubbed and constantly replaced every twelve hours. Rumor had it that during the Cuban missile crisis in 1962 President Kennedy took refuge here.

The Greenbrier was where de-facto President Valerie Clay now presided over the United States.

Captain Mike Desantos, flanked by the surviving members of his Delta Team, ducked his head and rapidly covered the distance from the Pave Hawk to the group awaiting them.

President Clay was flanked by her Secret Service Detail. It consisted of four fit looking men with SCAR machine guns at the ready, heads swiveling on the lookout for any threats. Each man had an earpiece and the obligatory dark sunglasses.

Valerie Clay was still getting used to being POTUS. She reached out her hand only to be greeted by textbook salutes from the operators.

TRUDGE: SURVIVING THE ZOMBIE APOCALYPSE

Well, I am the Commander in Chief now. President Clay reciprocated to the best of her ability and then got down to business.

"Captain Desantos, you were tasked to retrieve the football because we have reason to believe the Chinese released the virus. Currently eight of our carrier groups are at sea. What is most distressing is that they are all being shadowed by the Chinese Navy's new submarine fleet. They have near silent hunter killers and have already used them to sink one of our boomers. I and the remaining brass believe this may go nuclear. As much as it's not the American way to strike first, it might be our only option."

"I know it's probably way above my pay grade, but how bad has China been affected by the virus or whatever it is?" Mike queried the new President.

"Just between you and I, we have lost all contact with our human intelligence on the ground. China has gone quiet as has most of the Asian continent. On the last nighttime pass our Keyhole satellite relayed imaging indicating massive power outages, even in Beijing. The last contact with our eyes on the ground was day one of the infection here stateside. He indicated the government had gone underground and most of the population was being confined to their homes. The most chilling intel he forwarded was that he had observed Chinese death squads shooting and bagging anyone in the streets."

"First of all, with all due respect, Madam President, the death squads were culling the infected... right?"

"No, our man said that the majority of the people killed in the first wave were all healthy citizens. The government knew how virulent the bug was that got away from them. Knowing how ruthless the Chinese are, they were just being proactive. Hey, they've done it before... albeit on a much smaller scale."

"Well then, why on earth would they want to attack us with their superbug, why not just use a nuke or an electromagnetic pulse?"

"As the saying goes soldier, misery loves company. The agent, we'll call him Buddha, mentioned the city of Xinxiang as being the epicenter of their outbreak. Curiously enough that's where a major bioweapons lab is located. His Intel also suggests that they sent sixteen credentialed Chinese national couriers with diplomatic pouches to multiple cities in the continental United States. Four of

166

the couriers apparently arrived in DC just hours before the first confirmed cases of what the CDC in Atlanta has taken to calling the "Omega Virus."

"What does the CDC have to say about this Omega Virus?"

President Clay put her hands over her face for a short while. When she brought them down and looked at Mike she was speechless for a moment. Tears welled in her eyes as she recounted the staggering numbers of dead and infected Americans.

"The Center for Disease Control estimates the CONUS will be depopulated by ninety-five percent..."

"Forgive me Ma'am. You said depopulated. Didn't you mean repopulated... by the walking dead?"

"They assume that the risen will lose their ability to walk as they decompose and therefore after a few weeks they won't be able to infect any more of the population," the President said, staring off towards the 18th hole.

Mike noticed that she had developed the thousand yard stare a person acquires when they had seen too much in too short a time.

"You know that old saying, what is the definition of assume?"

The new President testily answered, "Assuming makes an ass out of you and me... what is your point, soldier?"

"Until I see one of those dirty walking corpses die from anything but a bullet to the brain, I will take *nothing* for granted."

"I agree. For now your main objective is containment, followed by securing all of the information about Omega that we can," President Clay said.

"What are my orders now?" Captain Desantos asked.

"I need you to take your team to the CDC in Atlanta and collect any living personnel, the research notes and any samples they have archived and then escort them to Schriever Air Force base. Use force if necessary. Capture, don't kill."

"Yes Madam President, anything else?"

"I have bad news. While you were in transit from the White House I was informed of Fort Bragg's dire situation. The base is surrounded and under siege and waiting for a full airlift. Any personnel that get out before the undead overrun the base are going to rendezvous at Schriever AFB. The 50th space wing controls all the Department of Defense satellites from that location. We are going to reestablish the United States government and the CDC in Colorado Springs."

Her last few words garbled together as Mike thought about his family and unborn son. Hopefully they all would be reunited soon. In a moment of clarity he also thought about Brook and Raven. They were like family to him. An icy fist hit him in the gut as he calculated the odds of all of them surviving.

President Clay gave one last salute to the men in front of her and then approached the operator that had retrieved the football hours earlier. She reached out and removed the Captain's bars from Mike Desantos' uniform, replacing them with the silver two star cluster of a Major General's rank.

Mike remained stoic. He saluted the President, turned and reentered the waiting helo. Engines spooled up and the four birds leapt off of the beautiful country club-like grounds and accelerated to maximum speed, heading for another much needed aerial refueling before setting waypoints for Atlanta.

Chapter 36
Day 2 - Fort Bragg, North Carolina

Their vantage point afforded them a view of the north gate and watchtowers. A large brown wooden sign with the words "*Fort Bragg, Home to the 82nd Airborne and Special Forces, Welcome*" carved into it loomed next to the entrance. Three fifty-foot tall guard towers spanned the front of the base with a fifteen foot tall chain-link fence capped by razor sharp concertina wire ringing the entire facility. There were hundreds of the walking dead milling about or trying to gain entrance; the moaning was loud enough to be heard at their semi-secure location half a mile away. The blood slickened grass in front of the fencing was littered with the bodies of fallen undead; some still moved and clawed their way mindlessly towards the living. Every few seconds one or two of the undead would suddenly collapse, unmoving, felled by the snipers in the towers.

Fort Bragg was a huge base sprawling over several thousand acres. From one corner of the base thick black smoke curled up into the crystal clear blue sky. Very far off, what appeared to be a large cargo or transport plane orbited, belching solid streams of red tracers groundward. It appeared that unbroken chains of light anchored the plane to the ground. This effect was due to the high rate of fire coming from the multiple Gatling guns as they rained tracer bullets down into the masses of undead. Thankfully the wind was at their backs, as it helped to drown out the incessant, maddening sounds coming from below; also it helped carry the zombies' rancid odor elsewhere.

Brook opened the emergency medical kit Carl had procured from the store in Laurinburg and was busy dabbing Neosporin on her brother's face. She was not new to this; Brook was an ER nurse back in Portland and knew how to treat all but the most severe of wounds. She had picked out the bits and pieces of small buckshot and glass she could get ahold of with the cheap tweezers that came with the kit.

"Ow… take it easy Nurse Ratchett!"

"Then quit yer movin', gunslinger," Brook said in her best Rooster Cogburn.

"Hey, I got the job done didn't I? Last time I checked that monster stopped walking."

"OK. Good shooting Tex," Brook conceded as she finished her field surgery.

She left Carl's face exposed. It would heal much faster in the open air, but it had immediately started to bleed again after the antibiotic was applied.

"In an hour or so it should start to scab. Just keep away from the walkers. The last thing you want to do is get any of their saliva in your open wounds."

Brook asked the boy if she could put some antibiotic on his burn. The boy silently looked at her.

"What's your name?"

In fractured English dripping with a Russian accent the boy said "Dimitri" and nothing else.

Resigned to the fact that he had been through a hell of an ordeal on top of the gift shop back in Aberdeen, she figured he would get over the sunburn.

While Brook had been tending to her brother's mangled face, Raven stood watch. There were a few of the walking dead but they largely ignored the little group and instead were drawn to the gunfire and display of aerial firepower.

Carl had parked the Raptor at the base of a tall white water tower; it was elevated and provided an unobstructed view of the north side of the base. Because the tower and its associated outbuildings were protected by the same type of fence as the base, forced entry was necessary. One push with the brush guard of the Raptor made the locked gate spring inward. Once the truck was inside of the chain-link fence, Brook leapt out and coiled the remaining pieces of the newly broken chain around the two halves of the gate. One or two of the walkers wouldn't push it in, but a large mass of them was another story.

Down below, bodies were piling up four and five deep outside of the gates. Three cars had just driven up to the entrance and the occupants hurriedly piled out. The volume of gunfire increased; eight people in all were fighting for their lives. A short, stocky man fired his pistol point blank into the throng of walkers. Several fell, but their sheer numbers overwhelmed him. Even from this far away his shrieks were audible as the man was eaten by the undead. Two ghouls fought over his entrails, playing a sickening game of tug of war. His death created a momentary diversion. The rest of the group huddled near the closed gate, pleading desperately to be let inside. Gunfire rained down from the guard towers in a renewed frenzy. The advancing walkers fell in bloody heaps here and there. A lone soldier fumbled with the locks. Finally the gate parted wide enough to allow five of the survivors to enter. The undead overwhelmed the last two men. The monsters tore them limb from limb, the ghouls fighting over each appendage like dogs wrestling over a prized bone. Hair raising, blood curdling screams lasted a few short seconds only to be drowned out by the ever-present moans coming from the rotting mass of walking corpses. Brook shook her head in dismay for those men that hadn't made it, but thought it was commendable that the soldiers were risking their own lives for a handful of living breathing citizens.

Carl pointed at the group of abandoned cars and told Brook his incredibly dangerous but well thought out idea.

"Do you see the black car in the back, the one pushed up against the red truck that's lodged next to the fence?"

"Yes what about them?" Brook went along trying to figure out where he was going with this.

"Did you ever watch the Dukes of Hazard?" Carl asked, looking at his sister.

A look of knowing apprehension crossed Brook's face. "Are you going to try and jump the fence?"

"Not exactly. I think with the number of those things on the ground down there, we can drive over them and up onto the back of that black car and use it as a ramp…"

Brook cut him off. "Even if you drive up onto those cars and reach the fence, those stinking fuckers will tear us apart like they did those poor souls a minute ago."

Ignoring her, Carl continued. "We will be up out of their reach, and then I will make a stirrup with my hands." Putting his hands together, showing Brook what he meant. "Then after we crest the stalled cars you three can climb right over."

"A lot can go wrong."

"Do you have a better idea Sis? The way I see it, things are only going to get worse across the country. That means there are millions of those things between here and Oregon. At least once inside maybe we can hitch a ride on one of the helicopters to someplace safe."

"Go through the sunroof," said a voice from out of nowhere.

Everyone turned their heads at once and looked at Dimitri.

"What did you say?" Carl asked.

"Go through the sunroof…" this time barely audible but with a distinctive Slavic accent, he was a shy kid it seemed.

"Hell of an idea kid," Carl replied, his head nodding up and down in agreement.

Everyone piled into the Ford pickup before Carl started the noisy engine. Slowly he backed through the gate; Brook closed it after them and reentered the vehicle. Goosing the powerful motor, Carl followed the access road back to the main artery leading to Fort Bragg. The guard house had long ago been abandoned and the entrance had been shored up with concrete jersey barriers. The front grass and flower beds were fully covered with vehicles of all shapes and sizes. Scores of the undead had clambered up onto the raft of idle cars, fallen into crevices between the gridlocked vehicles and then became trapped. Charting a course through the hundreds of walkers, Carl found his makeshift ramp. The black Ford Crown Victoria was nosed into the back of a host of smaller vehicles that were in turn nestled up to the red truck. The snipers above had apparently favored the area behind that particular group of cars as their killing grounds. Undead were stacked upon each other, three feet deep, like cordwood.

He slowed the off-road vehicle to a crawl, put the truck into four wheel drive and locked the differential. Brook pumped shell after shell from the Mossberg through her open window putting down the nearest threats, pausing only to reload. The knobby front tires bit into the putrid flesh pile and powered up onto the back of the Crown Vic. The car's roof creaked and the windows simultaneously exploded; the truck settled in but kept moving forward. From the pockets in the sea of abandoned cars, undead reached up, grasping at the moving vehicle. Chunks of rotten meat the size of softballs spewed from the rear of the Raptor. The mud flaps were covered with a sheen of blood and other fluids.

Carl maneuvered the truck up the metal Matterhorn. The smaller compact cars collapsed under the weight as the truck kept creeping towards the perimeter fence. Sniper fire again picked up in intensity. A large pack of walkers milled on both sides of the abandoned cars and trucks, and they began falling in greater numbers. The Raptor's huge off road tires sank into the roofs of a Honda Civic and a tiny Mini Cooper; the truck wallowed, seemingly stuck while the entranced horde crushed inward. Dimitri was lying on the back seat, not wanting to see what he was hearing outside of the steel cocoon. Raven held her nose and kept her eyes glued forward, imposing a mental blindfold on herself. The sounds of the dead drowned out the straining power plant as Carl coaxed the truck over this last hurdle; they had just been in the trough, now they all faced the crest of the sea of vehicles. A blood and gore smeared, yellow Hummer2 sat sideways. Its boxy body was smashed up against the imposing razor wire topped fence. Burnt rubber and the smell of hot oil from the overworked engine intermingled with the sickly sweet smell of death. As the bright orange truck scaled the Hummer2, Carl opened the electric moon roof. Brook retrieved the two empty duffel bags they had stolen from the Bi-Mart. The final obstacle was the razor sharp coil of concertina wire looming above them.

"Get ready to go out through the moon roof when I say go!" Brook yelled over the laboring V8 as she held on for dear life. A spontaneous cheer sounded for the survivors. The soldiers on the ground moved along the inside of the fence line to receive them once they safely made it over. The truck lost out to gravity and ground to a halt at a forty five degree angle. Its spinning tires had left dark black rubber marks along the side of the yellow Hummer2 it now rested atop.

Brook crawled out through the moon roof with Raven and Dimitri close behind; she draped the two empty duffel bags across the concertina wire before putting her hands clasped together in front of the kids. Raven stepped up and Brook launched her over the top of the wire. The soldiers on the other side handily broke her fall as the entire group broke out with another boisterous round of cheers and applause. Dimitri had to be put over the top forcibly by Brook. He was kicking and screaming; he obviously didn't like heights. The young boy fell into the hands below. His landing was harder than Raven's and he cried out in pain. Considering their unraveling situation at the base, saving the two kids provided inspiration for the besieged troops. The loud cheering continued.

Meanwhile Carl struggled to force his large frame through the opening in the roof. He steadfastly urged his sister to go on without him. Brook pulled unsuccessfully on his outstretched arms before she finally relented and continued on. She leapt from the roof of the truck aiming for the shredded black bags. She landed partially on top of the hastily covered razor wire and bellied over, suffering severe gashes on both arms and torso, before tumbling safely amongst the soldiers below.

Specialist Jack Bowers watched the proceedings through his high powered scope. His brow furrowed when he got a clear look at what was trying to wriggle through the sunroof of the high centered 4x4. It appeared to be one of the infected. The trigger pull of his rifle was set to two and a half pounds and his finger currently held it at two. Breathing in and then slowly exhaling, he readied for the shot. High caliber ammunition was in short supply and since no one was in immediate danger he backed off the shot, leaving the kill for the troops on the ground. *Pretty fluid movement for a walker,* he thought as he watched the thing clamber over the wire, waiting for the volley of gunfire that would end its miserable existence. The soldier shuddered at the thought of coming back as one of them. He would rather use a Claymore mine for a pillow than walk the earth in search of human flesh.

Carl had fared much better when he dropped into the store through the skylight. This time he fell awkwardly, the soldiers all standing back not wanting to touch the bloody scab-faced thing coming over the fence. Not certain if he was infected or not, they let him fall to the ground.

"He's one of us! He is not infected!" Brook shrieked as the soldiers brought their arms to bear. Carl's ankle was bent at an unnatural angle; he let out a yelp of pain, followed by a profanity-laced tirade.

"Would it have been too much to ask of you to break my fall? Goddamn, motherfucker, shit…! I think my ankle is broken!"

The man nearest to Carl slowly lowered his rifle. "That's the least of your problems. You should see your face." The rest of the soldiers, knowing full well that the undead didn't curse, put their muzzles down and rushed to his aid.

Chapter 37
Day 3 - Outskirts of Boise, Idaho

The radio in Harry's hand crackled to life.

"Harry, Duncan, anyone there? This is Cade."

"Copy that, this is Harry. We have been trying to get ahold of you since we heard the explosions. What happened?"

"Someone had a gas leak," Cade said, tongue firmly planted in cheek.

"Helluva lot of gas my friend. Are you OK?"

"Fit as a fiddle. I'm almost to your position. Did you two have any visitors?"

Harry replied, "The walkers have been arriving in trickles from the east. There is an immense wall of smoke in the direction of Boise. It looks like a forest fire... only there are white and black oily looking plumes roiling up."

"Boise is on fire," Cade said matter-of-factly, his real voice mingled with the sound emanating from the radio as he emerged out of the woods just feet from Harry.

He was greeted by back slaps and smiles. "Quite a few of those dirtbags met their maker; I guess we got a little retribution for our friend's deaths. It still doesn't feel right killing the living... considering how few of us there are left," Cade said, his voice trailing off as he strode to a clearing to look east towards Boise.

Columns of different colored smoke dotted the horizon from north to south as far as the eye could see. In the failing light oranges and reds from the fires created a false sunset from the direction the sun always made its appearance.

"We have two choices. One, go back the way we came and cross back into Oregon then drive south to the Nevada border. Or…" he turned and pointed to Boise, "take our chances that we don't run into anything fleeing the fires, living or undead."

"I vote for Boise…" His movement was a blur; Cade drew the Glock 17 from his thigh holster and swept the muzzle towards Duncan. Six rapid shots later three undead lay still and bleeding from a double tap to the head each. Harry and Duncan, slack-jawed and wide-eyed, stared at the man who had just fired six bullets through the air that separated them.

"Why didn't they moan before they got that gosh darn close?" Harry asked, white as a sheet from the sudden action and the proximity of speeding lead to his cranium.

"Good God damn shooting," Duncan added in his usual raspy drawl.

Two of the cadavers looked as if they had been among the first undead to turn. They were fully into the process of decay. Their flesh was a mottled gray, covered with pustules and boils. Their hair had fallen out in clumps, giving them a punk rock look. Their clothing was that of serious hikers: boots, cargo shorts and Gore-Tex. The third walker used to be a soldier. He had no hair but looked to have been dead only a day or two. He had a patch on his ACUs that read *Paulson*; his former rank was Corporal in the Idaho National Guard.

"I haven't a clue why they didn't moan like usual. I do hope, however, they aren't learning new hunting techniques. We had better get going." Cade walked to his truck. Harry had a hard time moving as he was still in a little bit of shock from the incident moments ago. His hands were also shaking from the sudden, intense rush of adrenaline.

*****

They didn't even bother to finish their vote. Duncan followed the Sequoia towards the smoke and flames. The road was clear for the first ten miles and then there were wrecks and clogs of stalled cars scattered here and there. No sign of living humans was evident. Deer, raccoon and other wildlife were on the move away from the direction the two vehicle convoy headed. The nearer they got to the city, the more of the undead they encountered. Some were blackened and sooty, flesh sloughing off of them, but still they walked. The crispy ghouls were reaching and swiping at the trucks as they passed, leaving slimy black traces anywhere they made contact.

Cade slowed up ahead and drove over two of the brittle walkers before stopping completely, engine still idling.

Duncan followed his lead. From the cab of the truck, Harry had to shoot two advancing walkers with his pump shotgun before he could safely call Cade on the Motorola. The men watched as Cade gophered his head up through the moon roof of the Sequoia. Four undead changed course and ambled towards the idling truck. Cade put them down with his M4; more were on the way from their front and sides. The undead started moaning as they drew nearer. Cade dropped his rifle, letting it hang on its sling and brought the binoculars to his eyes glassing the road ahead.

The radio chirped in Cade's pocket. "What do you see, boss?"

Keying the mike, Cade replied, "About a mile ahead. There's a helicopter blocking the road... and lots of undead between us and it."

Duncan motioned for the radio. Harry handed it over.

"This is Duncan. If it still has electrical and fuel, I think I can fly that bird."

Since there would be plenty of paper laying around if they all survived the day, Cade jokingly made Duncan an offer he couldn't refuse.

"Roger that. I'll pay you ten million dollars if you can fly us out of this predicament."

"You got it big spender," Duncan replied, knowing full well his chain was being yanked. He disappeared back into his truck, tromped the gas pedal and left black stripes on the sun-bleached gray asphalt as he hauled ass towards the helicopter.

They plowed over as many of the walking dead as they could on the way to the grounded helo.

*****

Duncan had been mentally going through preflight checklists from decades ago. The helicopter sitting in front of them was a Utah

Air National guard UH-60 Black Hawk. It appeared air worthy but the pilot was still strapped in, dead and slumped over the controls.

To Cade's trained eye, judging by the different types of spent shell casings, it was apparent this ambush was orchestrated by the same group that killed Rawley, Leo and Sheila. The ambush victims' bodies were placed in a row behind the burned out hulk of a Humvee. The naked corpses had high and tight haircuts, and all of the bodies still had dog tags around their necks as well. Two of the troops had been hit in the head by a large caliber weapon and had most likely died instantly. The other two men weren't as lucky; they had been tortured. Their bodies were covered with purple welts and crisscrossed with deep cuts. Both soldiers had their necks cut ear to ear and one of the men had a large swastika gouged into his chest.

Peeling his eyes from the dead servicemen, he could feel the anger and hatred towards the despicable men that had committed these acts welling up in him. *No sense living in the past. Those bastards already paid for this.* Cade turned his attention to their escape.

"Well, can you fly this model?" he asked Duncan with a concerned look on his face.

"If it spools up, I can fly the bird. They all have the same controls, a collective/throttle, cyclic and anti-torque pedals. No problem," Duncan said, sounding more confident than he really was.

Duncan left his pickup on the shoulder of the road and grabbed the shotgun and the backpack containing his few personal belongings. On the lookout for undead, he cautiously covered the distance to the helicopter. The road weary veteran heaved his pack into the crew compartment of the Black Hawk. With a heavy heart he looked at the man still strapped in the gurney. He had been dead for some time and was most likely the patient the medevac chopper had been summoned for in the first place. Duncan hauled his old frame up into the cramped confines of the Black Hawk. With Harry's help they removed the gurney to free up room.

Duncan placed the corpse on the ground near the others. The fire in the distance loomed larger on the horizon and loud cries of the dead carried forth, riding the hot desert wind. Duncan returned to the grim task of removing the pilot's body. After making sure that he was indeed dead, Duncan unbuckled his safety harness and gently, out of respect for the man in uniform, carried him to the roadside and lowered him to the ground next to the other dead soldiers. Duncan unclasped the chin strap and removed the flight helmet from the fallen aviator. He stood back a step and gave the slain men a final crisp salute. *The dead that stay dead really are the fortunate ones. When will the madness end?* he thought, shedding a rare tear. It was a very poignant moment for Harry and Cade who looked on from a distance.

Duncan worked to figure out the helicopter's intricate avionics. The Hueys he used to fly in Viet Nam were like Model T's compared to this UH-60.

Cade hastily assembled the sniper rifle and scanned the oncoming highway and surrounding woods. He searched for the source of the moans; they had been growing louder by the minute. A lone, partially clothed figure shuffled through the shimmering thermal distortion cast up from the hot blacktop. The female walker had a half limping, part shuffling gait, her bare breasts keeping cadence with her flopping head. She looked like a marshmallow left in the fire too long. Cade rested the cross hairs on the crispy critter's brow; milky white eyes stared through what remained of the charred face. Slowly he pulled the trigger. The ghoul's head split down the middle and like a cracked egg, her cooked brain slid out. At once another walker took her place.

Harry and Cade kept up their steady firing, thinning out the advancing undead.

Duncan swore as he scanned the multitude of switches which glowed in muted reds and greens. Thankfully the helicopter did have electrical power and the main fuel gauge registered one quarter of a full load. Duncan guessed they would have a hundred mile range, maybe two.

Harry fired the SKS at the army of undead. The familiar sound was reassuring to Cade's ears, even if it was Harry wielding the weapon. Switching from the sniper rifle to his M4 allowed Cade a greater rate of fire. The undead were now piling up in a semi-circle flanking the helicopter. After an agonizingly long wait the turbine finally whined to life. Looking over his shoulder Cade saw the rotor blades spooling up and a grinning Duncan triumphantly flashing him a thumbs up.

Cade sprinted to the vehicles to begin transferring the guns and supplies. The distinctive sonic cracks from bullets whipping by his head got his undivided attention. Someone was shooting at them. Using his truck for cover, he looked through the windows in the direction he thought the fire had come from. There were several motorcycles and a bright yellow civilian Hummer2 closing on them from the west. The shooter was hanging out of the moving Hummer's passenger window.

Cade slapped a fresh magazine in the carbine and aimed at the windshield of the Hummer. Two controlled bursts from the M4 spider webbed the glass on the driver's side. This caused the big SUV to swerve and careen over three of the motorcycles, pulping the riders on the pavement, before rolling in a bright yellow blur of exploding glass and scraping metal.

The rest of the motorcycles stopped in the middle of the road; the riders dismounted and crouched behind their Harleys. The silhouette of a man shouldering a very long rifle presented itself in front of the setting sun. A hand grabbed Cade's shoulder and pulled him towards the noisy Black Hawk. Cade spun and followed with only his M4 to show from his aborted trip to the vehicles. Harry turned about and hobbled to the big helicopter. Both men climbed aboard and strapped themselves into jump seats in the open passenger compartment.

The smell of the Black Hawk's exhaust and the odor of the dead assailed their nostrils. Bullets were beginning to impact the fuselage, metallic pings sounding as Duncan twisted the throttle and applied full power. The Black Hawk bolted into the darkening cobalt sky at ten feet a second. Harry wasn't used to the sensation of lift off. Feeling green and awash in nausea, he fired the last of his ammo at the ghouls. The ground rushed away, unfortunately the dead didn't. One of the undead had gotten both hands wrapped around one of the wheel struts. Harry fired at the top of its head, causing the creature to lose purchase. He looked on with grim satisfaction as it freefell one hundred and twenty feet to earth, leaving a grimy crater in the desert soil.

Even though he knew they were at max range for the carbine, Cade continued firing at the bikers until his magazine was empty and the bolt locked open.

*****

On the ground below Richard Ganz, leader of the Nomad Jesters, was on bent knee steadying the Barrett sniper rifle across the handlebars of his Harley. His target was the man piloting the helicopter. He smoothly increased tension on the trigger, the bullet left the muzzle at 2800 feet a second and passed harmlessly under the fuselage. Ganz chambered another round, steadied and took another shot. The result was the same; the helicopter was now too far away, even for the sniper rifle. Enraged, Ganz pulled his Desert Eagle Magnum from the leather holster on his hip and shot his newest prospect point blank in the head. The big biker's temper was legendary. He led the Jesters with an iron fist and was indiscriminate in who he killed before the breakdown of society. Now he had no one to answer to and his tantrums went unchecked.

The young prospect lay in the middle of the highway bleeding from the head and slowly turning pale. Ganz mounted his Harley, kick started it and headed away from the advancing ghouls. Left with little choice, the remnants of his gang followed.

*****

Duncan threw the co-pilot's helmet to Cade and pointed out the others hanging next to the medical litters. Cade plugged the flexible coiled wire into the comms jack on the bulkhead above him. Harry followed suit and plugged in after donning a helmet. Duncan's voice came through loud and clear in both men's helmets. "We were between the proverbial rock and a hard place back there. Thank God for Igor Sikorsky."

"Did any of their gunfire damage the helo?" Cade asked.

"Doesn't feel like it. Why? Are we leaking something I can't see?"

"No, just checking. I felt bullets impacting as we lifted off."

"I'll watch the gauges closely. Cade, what do you know about these newfangled radios?" Duncan asked with a hint of exasperation showing in his voice.

Working the seatbelt buckles loose, Cade said "I'm going to unstrap and move into the copilot's seat. Hold her level and steady."

"I think it's all coming back to me now. Kinda like riding a bicycle, you know."

"What now guys?" Harry asked through the inflight communications.

Ignoring Harry, Duncan shouted "Hallelujah my fellow flying friends. I just realized what an ERFS is."

"I'm sitting on pins and needles... enlighten us" Cade said.

"While I thought we had about two hundred miles of range, I was mistaken. When I flip this switch..." Duncan paused for effect.

"Just spit it out man," Harry said sounding a little pissed off.

Duncan spoke. "Those stubby wings on the side of her usually hold guns and missiles, but this is a dust-off bird equipped with extra external fuel tanks. Voilà!" Duncan exclaimed as he flipped the switch labeled ERFS and added, "We now have an extremely extended range."

The last two days were taking a toll on Harry. Being retired, he was used to not having to answer to anybody. Solitude was what he now craved. Where Harry came from, a sixty-five-year-old man was asked to share his wisdom. He hated being ignored and made to feel like he was six. *Oh well, if they don't value my wisdom, then screw the know-it-alls.* His feelings were hurt so he clammed up for the rest of the flight.

Cade found his way into the co-pilot's seat and was manipulating the knobs and buttons on the military radio. He looked like he knew what he was doing as he tried to pick up anyone that might be listening in on any of the usual emergency bands.

For five minutes they listened in as the former Delta Operator attempted to contact any available U.S. forces. He left the radio on the Military band reserved for aviation assets and then focused on programming waypoints into the navigation computer. Remembering how to use the nav gear came back a little slower than the comms gear.

"Where to boss?" the Viet Nam-era aviator asked.

"Follow the waypoints I just plotted on your HUD (heads up display) and we'll be flying over..." he was about to say Boise until Duncan banked the Black Hawk and he actually saw what was left of the city. Boise resembled the old pictures he had seen depicting Japan after the firebombing campaigns of World War II.

The sky was filled up to their altitude with black feathery ashes and fires raged everywhere. The helicopter moved along at an altitude of five hundred feet. The multitudes of undead surging west were clearly visible to the naked eye. The three men were speechless as they flew over what was left of the Idaho Air National Guard base. Three helicopters were burned to the tarmac, fixed in place by melted tires; the skeletal remains of the titanium airframes resembled the tangled wreckage of the zeppelin Hindenburg. Quonset huts burned, the vehicles parked nearby further fueling the inferno. Airmen and women lay where they had fallen, some having been consumed by the shambling packs of ghouls. The few vehicles moving below were fleeing the conflagration in front of the walkers. The scope of the damage was unimaginable. The city now belonged to the dead.

*****

Cade changed the waypoints in the flight computer. The new course would take them along the Wasatch mountain front. The towering crags ran north/south, flanking Salt Lake City, Utah.

"The 19th Special Forces Group is located in Draper, Utah. I set the waypoints to take us there. I know a few of the operators garrisoned at the base. At the very least we may be able to top off and continue onward."

"If the base is still standing when we get there, I think it's the end of the road for me, fellas," the usually quiet Harry said over the intercom.

"I'm sure we can get you set up with supplies and transportation, if you really don't want to stick around," Cade said, without a trace of emotion. He had a hard and fast rule to not form emotional attachments to anyone but family. Kids were the one exception and he had felt the pain from it these last twenty-four hours. Leo and more so the younger Ike had really grown on him. There would be time to grieve later... there always was.

Cade hadn't heard from his family for over two days now. He searched his pockets for his phone and remembered it and all of his gear, guns, ammo and food were abandoned with their vehicles outside of Boise. All he had was his M4 with one mag left, a Glock pistol, the clothes and combat gear he still wore as well as his helmet. It dawned on him his favorite Trailblazer ball cap was also in the Sequoia more than fifty miles away. He closed his eyes and visualized his wife's and daughter's faces in his mind. As darkness enveloped Idaho, the desert air whipping in the open troop compartment grew measurably colder. Despite the temperature change a warm feeling washed over Cade. There was a special bond that held his small family together, through overseas deployments and other unforeseen hardships; he knew beyond a shadow of a doubt they still lived.

Cade kept watch out of the co-pilot seat. He hadn't seen this many stars since he was a member of Task Force-121. It had been a handpicked group of operators hunting for Osama Bin Laden in the Hindu Kush Mountains of Afghanistan. The high altitude and inhospitable terrain that they operated in left him with very few pleasant memories; the stars were one of them. He glanced into the mirror affixed above the cockpit glass. A breathtaking display of purple and magenta painted the sky behind them and reflected off of the Black Hawk's windows. The sun was going down slowly, kicking and screaming as if it didn't want to leave the living alone in the dark with the dead.

Looking groundward, it suddenly dawned on him there was an absence of light below and there were no moving vehicles. Mother Nature's beautiful sky show belied the fact the world was ending, not with a bang, but a whimper. Cade thought, *T.S. Eliot surely knew something we didn't.*

Duncan's Southern drawl sounded in his ear and brought him back to reality.

"Look off to the right at 2 o'clock. Do you see it?"

"Yeah, it looks like a small sun," was Cade's reply.

Duncan banked the helo to the right and aimed the nose toward the brilliant lights.

Chapter 38
Day 2 - Fort Bragg, North Carolina

Carl narrowly escaped death, first from the fall and then at the hands of the United States Special Forces troops. Until today he had no idea the fear six machine gun muzzles could invoke in a man, especially if they all were pointed at him. The injuries to his face were superficial and his ankle had been reset and put in a walking cast. His next major hurdle was infection. The ghoul that clawed up his back had given him several different types of disease. He was mildly sedated and sleeping. Brook and Raven held a bedside vigil.

Outside the battle raged on. The steady small arms gunfire and the constant booming from the side-mounted 105mm Howitzer on the circling C-130 Spectre gunship both comforted and scared Brook at the same time. She was crossing a line that usually took most soldiers a stint in boot camp, and at least a couple of firefights to even approach. Her senses were being fine-tuned and honed. Until now they were strictly tools of basic survival. Now she possessed a combination of aggression, assertiveness and self-preservation. Slowly the old Brook was being reforged and transformed. Gone was the survivor's guilt. The time for surviving was now. Raven depended on her.

*****

Their weapons were all confiscated and then the group was immediately escorted to the base's medical facilities. A man in full combat gear walked them towards the middle of Fort Bragg. On the way he told them they needed a cursory exam to ensure nobody was seriously injured going over the wire.

Carl's wounds were completely scrubbed, disinfected and bandaged. A big burly male nurse cleaned and sutured the lacerations on Brook's arms and abdomen. The exams were thorough, any idiot would know they were being screened for infection and checked for bites, even though it wasn't divulged to them. Dimitri was not talking and Brook guessed the little boy was suffering from PTSD. One of the doctors wheeled him to an infirmary elsewhere to be attended to. They were all going to be quarantined for twenty-four hours. Raven seemed depressed and was badly in need of some rest. Brook was just plain exhausted. Every nerve ending was shot. Brook took Raven's hand and led her down the hall to the room that had been assigned to them.

*****

Carl finally awoke and was reading a magazine. It was the last Newsweek ever; the cover read "Mad?? Disease." It was the last post-outbreak edition to be distributed and the words said it all. The Omega virus caught the entire United States flat footed and on the ropes. In the end, no one had enough time or information to stop it from spreading. Unable to keep his eyes open, Carl put the magazine down, closed his eyes and let sleep take over again.

*****

The first thing on Brook's agenda was to find Mike Desantos and ask him if he knew anything of Cade's whereabouts. She also had an irresistible urge to get out into the fight. This constant running and gunning had awakened something in her she didn't know existed. She craned her neck struggling to hear the new sounds outside of the door. Brook abruptly grabbed her daughter by the arm, shouldered the door open, burst out of their room and propelled her down the hall to where Carl was. The fusillade of automatic rifle fire sounded different, almost frantic. Dedicated, highly trained soldiers didn't lose their cool and "spray and pray."

They barged into the infirmary and Brook frantically yanked the IV tubes from her brother's arm. The sounds of the battle were drawing nearer and the undead's moaning was increasing in volume. Brook tried to wake Carl but he remained unresponsive. Shadows passed by the opaque green glass in the door and then stopped, wavering directly in front. Raven started whimpering; Brook pulled her close and clamped a hand over her mouth. Wild eyed and hyperventilating, she squirmed from her mom's grip and bolted for the hallway screaming. Brook suddenly became aware of the odor of rotting flesh overpowering the usual antiseptic hospital smell. The door burst inward followed by a torrent of decomposing corpses. They fell atop Raven, teeth gnashing, gnarled hands ripping the flesh from her face, exposing muscle, molars and jawbone. Blood pulsed onto the floor from hundreds of shredded capillaries. The room teemed with undead and they quickly turned their attention to the unarmed Brook. She braced herself and stood her ground in front of her unconscious and helpless brother.

*****

A shrill horn sounded. Brook awoke abruptly. Her chest heaved and she fought to breathe; beads of sweat cascaded from her face. Her thin hospital bed sheet was soaked through. Frantically she felt around in the dark and noisily exhaled when she felt the warmth of her daughter stir next to her. The nightmare was gone but the blaring klaxon was real.

Someone banged repeatedly on the door. Brook shook the sleep from her head, jumped to her feet and answered it.

The very pregnant Annie Desantos, her two young daughters flanking her, stood at the door's threshold and without entering told Brook and Raven the base was being evacuated.

"Are we leaving by air or land?" Brook queried her.

"Helicopters are inbound from Fort Campbell, women and children are assembling for evacuation first."

"I have to go get Carl. He's down the hall in the recovery ward. Can I leave Raven with you?"

Shaking her head, Annie said "No need, we're all going to the parade ground together. Chinooks are inbound to evac the wounded. Don't worry; the medical crew assured me they would accompany him."

"Raven, get your stuff. Annie, give us two minutes." Brook checked her phone once again. No bars, no message, no nothing. She sighed and threw the phone into her tote. They left the room hand in hand, following Annie and the girls. Cade was on Brook's mind.

*****

188

Fort Bragg was severely undermanned. Three-fourths of the active duty warfighters and base staff didn't return when they were recalled. A large contingent of Special Forces troops were still on deployment in Afghanistan and other unnamed places around the world.

During the night thousands of walking dead had encircled the entire perimeter. There were so many crushing together at the north gate, the cars and trucks left by the wire were being slowly compacted into the base of the fence. The orange Raptor precariously perched atop the Hummer2 finally succumbed to gravity and toppled to the ground, crushing a small number of the infected. The whole base was about to fall. Their sheer numbers were staggering. It was only a matter of time before they breached the fencing.

*****

The steady thumping of the dual rotor blade Chinooks helped drown out the sounds of the dead. While Brook was deep in the middle of her nightmare, their numbers had increased. The noise coming from their lifeless throats became an intolerable sonic tempest.

Annie had raided the shooting range for earplugs. Brook and Raven each had a pair of the little foam rubber plugs firmly embedded in their ears. Unfortunately they didn't keep out all of the noise.

Brook followed Annie and her girls along finely manicured paths that crisscrossed the base between buildings. Rotor wash and the accompanying flying debris blasted them as they rounded the corner. Shielding their faces with their hands, they approached the twin rotor behemoths, ducking instinctively. Annie and the girls took the last three spots in the crowded Chinook; they were sitting on the floor; nearby the loadmaster manned the mounted M240 machine gun.

Brook waved as the ramp partially lifted up. The hurricane-like winds increased as the helicopter powered up and rose into the sky. A soldier informed the waiting families that the next sortie of three helos was inbound and three minutes out.

The group of women and children nervously eyed the monsters crushing in on the perimeter fence. Ammunition was dangerously low; the troops had stopped shooting the undead outside

189

of the wire. Everyone prayed the fencing would hold up for another hour or two until the evacuation was complete.

The front fence failed first and the dead surged into the garrison parking lot. The first wave of them quickly overtook and consumed the guards and high ranking personnel in the nearby command post. Their screams were drowned out by the undead's eerie moaning.

Above the parade ground a large caliber rifle boomed from the guard tower. It was rhythmic and directed across the base to the south. The gunfire further aroused the dead and they started surging against the weakened barrier. Right on time the three CH-47 Chinooks thundered over the wire, flaring at the last second and softly settling to the ground. Rear and side doors opened up and the crew chiefs beckoned the people to hurry onboard.

The force of the surging undead finally caused the total failure of the perimeter fence. The sound of groaning metal preceded the collapse of the nearest guard tower. It listed and then toppled to the ground; the lone shooter went with it. Like piranhas the ghouls stripped the flesh from Jack Bowers' exposed extremities. Bloody hands reached under the ceramic-plated body armor and greedily scooped the soft organs from his abdomen. One of the dead picked up his rifle and peered down the still smoking barrel, determined it wasn't food and discarded it.

The rotor blades picked up speed; Brook sensed they weren't going to get aboard. She wondered if the nightmare had been a premonition of her death. A soldier fell ten feet from her, two of the monsters rending pieces of meat from his flailing arms and legs; he was close enough that Brook could hear his anguished wailing. The man lay still, his rifle near his body. She covered the ten feet in seconds and had the rifle in her hands before she was aware of her actions. The M4 barked twice, and the feeding creatures slumped atop their meal. More of them were now flanking the helicopter to the right. Taking careful aim with the weapon, Brook finished the nearest advancing walkers, dropping four in quick succession. With Raven in tow she boarded the hovering Chinook through the open side door. The monsters were grasping onto the rear ramp. The soldier manning the M240 now had a clear field of fire and started hammering away at them, the machine gun's report reminding Brook of a buzz saw ripping through wood. Rotor wash blew hot shell casings into the fuselage. A severely decomposed ghoul reached in and got ahold of Raven's ankle. Brook poked the M4s barrel past her daughter's body and emptied the last nine rounds into its head and chest. The zombie released its grip, fell twenty feet and disappeared into the sea of rotting corpses.

The Chinook left terra firma underneath it, nosed down and buzzed the building tops narrowly missing the south guard tower.

Not everyone made it out alive. The last helicopter to land took on passengers but the undead got aboard as well. The aviators lost control of the Chinook while trying to escape the attack. It took flight momentarily and then pitched over and rolled several times, pieces of rotor blade and bodies, human and undead, showering the parade grounds. Like army ants, thousands of the infected swarmed the few survivors that weren't killed outright in the violent crash. Fort Bragg fell to the dead three days after the Omega virus was released in the United States.

Chapter 39
Day 3 - 19th Special Forces Garrison, Draper, Utah

"God damn, they got that place lit up like Wrigley Field during a night game. Only I doubt they've got any peanuts... popcorn or crackerjacks."

Cade grinned. He kind of liked the pilot's gallows humor.

The base was visible for fifteen miles around.

"What you see is Camp Williams, 19th Special Forces garrison. Look for the parade ground or a training field for a landing spot, both should be lighted."

Duncan piped up over the intercom. "My boy, they have got that base so lit up, I don't think there is a nook or cranny where a shadow could hide."

Harry felt the Black Hawk slow and Duncan start the descent. It was evident why the base was awash in light.

"Holy mother of God" Harry exclaimed.

Cade had seen the same thing but his reaction was not a verbal one. By his estimation, there were hundreds of the creatures trapped in a massive trench running the length of the garrison. The closer they got to the parade ground the better he felt about what he was seeing. A blinding flash, followed by licking flames made Cade wince and cover his eyes. When he regained a semblance of normal night vision he could see multitudes of burning undead. The ghoul-filled slit carved into the earth was hard to comprehend.

"Hope y'all brought you some mustard... because we got us a weenie roast."

"Duncan, those used to be people. Can't you take this a bit more seriously? Maybe find a little sympathy for them?"

"Not a shred, Harry old boy. That's why I'm not going to be one of those critter's dinner. As we used to say in Nam, kill em all and let God sort em out."

As the Black Hawk made firm contact with the ground a shiver ran through the airframe.

"Been awhile hasn't it?"

"Cade, this ain't like riding a bicycle. The relearning curve is much steeper. Give me a few more hours and I'll have this whore doing back flips and landing on feathers."

Thinking he was stuck with a couple of frat boys, Harry muttered under his breath, "I'm through with you two jokers."

Duncan kept the rotorblades turning just in case they needed to effect a quick escape. Cade jumped out and sauntered, head ducked under the whirling rotor blades, towards the group of armed men heading his way. He knew the garrison commander from when he was with the 19th at Fort Lewis. Major Greg Beeson was a straight shooter (literally). He had trained snipers earlier in his career. They exchanged salutes and Cade asked him about the moat around the base.

"We had our engineers carve the trench with the dozers. When enough of the dead are assembled, a couple of boom boxes are set up near the pit, usually blaring heavy metal. They really love Metallica."

"That's what I call asymmetrical warfare," Cade quipped.

"It's pretty straight forward. They come in waves for some reason and so far they are pretty predictable. All we do is give it some time, and like lemmings, they do the rest."

They walked and talked. Cade explained how they came to possess the helicopter and who his travelling companions were, finishing with the bad news about Boise and the Air Guard base there. Cade cut to the chase and told his old instructor about his missing family and his unstoppable desire to locate them. Major Beeson informed Cade they had intercepted a call for help from Fort Bragg; it had been broadcast over the entire net. The base had been compromised and overrun. He didn't know about casualties, or how many had gotten out alive. The message gave no hint as to where the survivors, if any, were relocating to. After a long conversation Beeson indicated Cade could use any of the base assets to further his mission.

The Major offered sanctuary to Duncan and Harry. He told the aviator that he was welcome and his expertise was greatly needed. B Company was on deployment in Afghanistan when hell opened up and the dead arrived. Only half of C Company was able to return. Major Beeson was confident the base could hold its own as long as all of the undead residents of Draper didn't come calling. Duncan agreed to stay on, "For love of country" as he put it. Harry intended to leave at first light; he was feeling lonely, useless and a little restless. Not good for an old man's psyche.

Duncan ignored Cade's outstretched hand and instead embraced him in a surprise bear hug. Cade reciprocated, looked the old warhorse in the eyes and said a simple "Thanks."

Chapter 40
Day 3 - Sawtooth Mountains of Idaho

Mountain Man Dan, as the Stanley locals called him, pressed the binoculars to his face. He lived a solitary life up in the craggy Sawtooth Mountains. The area of the forest he called home was near an alpine lake at five thousand feet; he had been living here in the wild for the last sixteen years. Life had started closing in on him, or so he felt. It was too much for the old Vietnam vet to handle, when a sitting United States President got a hummer in the Oval Office and not a thing untoward happened to him. The bastard was even determined to grab for the guns of law abiding citizens while he tarnished the office and thumbed his nose at the Constitution. So Dan took his books and his guns and found his little slice of heaven.

He was in his element in the wilderness. Dan was a very patient and observant man. He always noticed anything out of the ordinary, and he had noticed that for the last three days there had been no air traffic. His first inclination was that the United States had suffered another 9/11 type terrorist attack.

The hike down to the small town usually took him four hours; a younger man could tackle it in two. The finger of rock he was perched on was only five feet across but it allowed him to stop and observe the last mile of the mountain trail he would have to descend.

The noises coming from below caught his attention before he even arrived at his usual resting spot. Gunfire echoed up from the Aryan Brotherhood camp. Dan witnessed the murder of four human beings in cold blood. The three men and a woman were dirty and shabbily dressed. One of the armed men released them from a building that looked like a tool shed or chicken coop. The four captives lurched into the middle of the compound. The shaved head, combat boot wearing skins were hooting and hollering while they stood in a semi-circle around the four people. Dan had a strong suspicion they were drugged because they staggered towards the assembled men in a lethargic, clumsy manner. He wasn't prepared for what happened next. The towering redhead stood apart from the rest. He pulled out a big chrome pistol and coldly shot the woman in the head. She fell to the dirt and ceased moving. The captive men didn't try to run, they just kept walking towards the pointed guns. As quick as it started it was over, AK-47s chattered and the three men dropped and sprawled on the ground, their blood turning the gravel black.

Dan wanted to go to town and tell Sherriff Blanda what he had just witnessed, but he couldn't risk being seen while trying to circumnavigate the compound. The redheaded biker was an affiliate of the Aryans and Dan had crossed paths with him on a number of occasions. Today he wanted no part of the murderer.

He was in no position to be a hero, so the mountain man silently reversed course and headed back to his remote cabin. Alone with his thoughts he started up the trail. *Those media folks will surely milk this latest terrorist attack for all it's worth. No doubt there will be old newspapers or magazines to read in town after this blows over.* Dan wasn't worried about a radiological dirty bomb affecting him here. *Why the hell would the idiots attack Idaho anyway? If this were another attack by Middle Eastern extremists then President Odero would have to listen to his fellow Americans and go kick some more Muslim ass.*

He really disliked this part of the climb. For every two steps forward, the surface underfoot shifted and put him one step backward. Head down, watching the trail while putting one foot in front of the other, Mountain Man Dan continued his long trudge back up his talus- and scree-covered mountain.

Epilogue
Day 4 - 19th Special Forces Garrison, Draper, Utah

The lemmings marched that morning. Cade, Duncan and Harry all slept in the same empty barracks. Slept was an overstatement. They were all awake when "Enter Sandman" commenced blaring from outside the fence. Because their numbers had steadily increased day by day the base commander made the decision to start eradicating the undead at first light and then again at dusk.

*****

Harry had taken up Major Beeson's offer of a taxpayer provided Ford F-350 pickup painted entirely in desert camouflage. A Mossberg 500 pump shotgun and a box of shells was provided by the base gunsmith. There was also a case of MREs sitting on the bench seat when Harry got in the truck. He was disappointed with himself because he didn't set out in search of his wife earlier and hated to admit he was scared of finding out what had really become of her. What Cade was doing was admirable and Harry used that example as motivation. He started the truck and waved halfheartedly towards Duncan and Cade. The perimeter outside the wire was momentarily free of undead. The soldiers opened the double gates for him.

No time like the present. Without looking back he maneuvered the ARMY 4x4 out of the compound and sped down the gravel road; dust billowed up, erasing the truck from view.

*****

The motorcycle Cade was given was an off road Kawasaki KLR 250. The bike was used by Delta Force, the 75th Rangers and many other Special Operations groups. While the civilian version proved to be very loud, the Special Ops build had beefier components and the exhaust was baffled for night time covert missions. While not entirely silent, it was extremely quiet and could go almost anywhere. Part of Cade's Ranger training included riding dirt bikes in extreme terrain. It had been years ago and there would be some rust to shake off. He had requested the dirt bike because it would use less gas and give him more range. Also the farther east he went the more road blockages he would probably be forced to navigate around. Since he had lost the match grade sniper rifle, Major Beeson had the armorer fit a silencer for the M4. The gun would be a bit harder to maneuver in close quarter battle, but the ability to kill quietly from a distance was well worth it. A new set of ACUs was offered and Cade donned the clean clothes, putting the rest of his gear in the saddle bags. Beeson gave him a few MREs and some bottles of water. The left saddle bag of the bike had been stocked with ammunition and extra magazines for his M4. In the right compartment was a small plastic gas can full of fuel and a length of hose for siphoning when necessary. The Major kept it short and told Cade he hoped he found his family safe and to be careful out there. The man handed him a small portable Sat phone with an extendable antenna.

"Use the usual escape and evade frequency if you get into trouble. If we have air assets, or can help in any way, we will. God speed, soldier." The men exchanged crisp textbook salutes.

Duncan approached Cade and handed him two metal canisters and a small red plastic gun. It was purple signal smoke and a Starlight flare gun. Duncan's usual gruff Southern drawl had a softer edge to it. "In case you get into trouble, mi amigo. Pop the purple haze and I'll know it's you. That is if I can get my hands on a bird." Before they parted ways, he tossed the young operator a set of the newest generation NVGs he had lifted from the Black Hawk.

The Kawasaki started right up and softly idled between Cade's legs. With the M4 stowed in a special compartment near his left leg and his trusty Glock holstered on his thigh, he engaged the clutch and then nudged the shifter into first gear.

The last few days had been a blur. Now when he tried to conjure the images of Raven and Brook from his memory the only faces that materialized were of the dead kids. Ike, Leo and the twins would not soon be forgotten. The world that they were supposed to inherit changed into one that snuffed the life from them. The former Delta Operator had all of the motivation he needed; he would see his family again. Fully aware of the ramifications and dangers he faced going it alone, Cade made the easy decision to trudge ahead. The bike's engine growled as he engaged the clutch. Without a backward glance he raced out of the gates and turned east on the gravel forest service road. Duncan watched until he disappeared into the woods and then listened to the bike's soft exhaust note until there was only silence.

# # #

Please join Cade's further adventures. The second installment of the Surviving the Zombie Apocalypse series, Soldier On: Surviving the Zombie Apocalypse, is now available. Thanks for reading! Shawn Chesser.

Feel free to find me on Facebook.

SHAWN CHESSER

ABOUT THE AUTHOR

Shawn Chesser, a practicing father, has been a zombie fanatic for decades. He likes his creatures shambling, trudging and moaning. As for fast, agile, screaming specimens... not so much. He lives in Portland, Oregon, with his wife, two kids and three fish. This is his first novel.

CUSTOMERS ALSO PURCHASED:

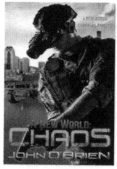

JOHN O'BRIEN
NEW WORLD
SERIES

JAMES N. COOK
SURVIVING THE DEAD
SERIES

MARK TUFO
ZOMBIE FALLOUT
SERIES

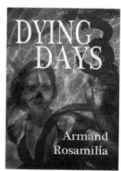

**ARMAND
ROSAMILLIA**
DYING DAYS
SERIES

HEATH STALLCUP
THE MONSTER
SQUAD

46190822R00117

Made in the USA
Middletown, DE
25 July 2017